The Urbana Free Library

To renew materials call
217-367-4057

S0-AGH-252

The Unholy Ghost

Also by Alistair Boyle

The

Unholy Ghost

A Gil Yates Private Investigator Novel

Alistair Boyle

ALLEN A. KNOLL, PUBLISHERS
Santa Barbara, CA

Allen A. Knoll, Publishers, 200 West Victoria Street,
Santa Barbara, CA 93101-3627
© 2003 by Allen A. Knoll, Publishers
All rights reserved. Published in 2003
Printed in the United States of America

First Edition

08 07 06 05 04 03   5 4 3 2 1

Library of Congress Cataloging-in-Publication Data

Boyle, Alistair.
   The unholy ghost : a Gil Yatse private investigator novel /Alistair Boyle. --1st ed.
      p. cm.
   ISBN 1-888310-67-7
   1. Yates, Gil (Fictitious character)--Fiction. 2. Private
investigators--California--Fiction. 3. Missing persons--Fiction. 4. California--Fiction. 5
Cults--Fiction. I. Title.

PS3552.O917U53 2003
813'.54--dc21   2002043331

Printed and bound by Sheridan Books, Ann Arbor, MI

text typeface is ITC Galliard, 12 point
printed on 60-pound acid free paper
Smyth sewn case bind with Skivertex Series 1 cloth

1

I didn't want to go, but I went. Why? The usual reason—money. I may not be cheap, but I can be bought. Lajos Bohem was doing the buying, and he could afford it. He made the movies the twelve year olds got such a kick out of: scantily clad bimbos, an automatic blazing in each hand, spewing endless fiery bullets as they leapt between skyscraper buildings.

Lajos Bohem; the Legend of Schlock.

In this business, you are bound to have clients you don't like. Bad things may happen to good people, but they also happen to bad people.

Lajos Bohem had bad things happen to him, but once you got to know him, it was impossible to feel sorry for him. He'd also had good things happen to him; that was what was so annoying. And the good things made him filthy rich. What made him so rich was an uncanny plug into the entertainment passions of the great unwashed masses—not surprising, since he had been one of them himself.

He was Hungarian and unpleasant. But the more I said "No," the more he sweetened the pot—

until the staggering mountain of possible cash over-whelmed me.

About the case he was a man possessed. I expect it was the same kind of passion that made him so successful in his trade. As successful as he was in his trade, he was a failure with his family—and being a man very much moved by appearances, it rankled, big time.

Lajos had a son who'd drugged himself to death. Lajos would claim that it was an accident, but it wasn't. His daughter Dawn had taken an easier way out—she joined one of those pop psychology pseudo religions called the Church of Technical Science—Techsci for short.

Seeing how happy Dawn was to be shut of old dad, his wife, Suzanne, also bailed the nest—under the guise of getting Dawn free of her demons. But something happened en route that made Suzanne see a different light. Rather than take Dawn back to Lajos, she joined the club herself, giving Lajos a double slap in the face.

His office was in the Mussolini-complex mode. His fatso desk was piled high with papers to give the impression he actually *did* something. Word in movie land was he simply counted the incidents of sex and violence in the scripts and made his decisions accordingly. It has been said you can't argue with success, but I'm sure whoever said that had not met Lajos Bohem.

There was a smile on his face as he saw me to my chair and circled the battlefield to sit himself in meglomania heaven.

"Thees man," Lajos said, gesturing helplessly with his hands, "thees phony hony man, Morgan, he is eevell. You weel find him for me, and I weel pay you veery good. And," he added as though he wanted to be sure I knew how important his loved ones were to him, "also, most important of course, my dear beautiful wife and daughter." He looked at the pictures he had prominently displayed on his desk, tilted so the visitors could see them. They were beautiful people. His wife had been a minor movie actress, and I don't think Lajos was at any pains to update the photograph. The daughter, too, was treated to a glamour pose. According to Lajos, daughter Dawn flew the coop for the sanctuary of Techsci in her late teens. Mom was well into her forties when she decided to join Dawn.

Looking at the picture of Suzanne, his wife, the word trophy came to mind. I imagined the trophy had become somewhat tarnished with time.

I was beginning to specialize in the tiered fee—the *modus* lent itself to cases of missing persons. So much dead, more alive, still more if a meeting is arranged.

Lajos Bohem had bucks, but one of the reasons he had so many of them was he knew how to hold onto them. Lajos was a master of the bait and switch, and I was lured into meeting after meeting with him on the pretense of his accepting my terms, only to find he'd found a new and creative way to chisel me. Each time I walked out, and each walkout was followed by a contrite, pleading phone call from Mr. Bohem.

Why did I keep bouncing back? I was intrigued by the case—though afraid of it. Plus, I was fascinated by Lajos Bohem himself. He was a man no one said no to. He had run roughshod over his business associates, investors, actors, directors, tradesman, craftsman and his family and girlfriends—I was just another blade of

3

grass he thought would bend in the wind, and if I
didn't he would trample me. Besides, if I worked it
right and covered my goal lines there was a big pot of
gold at the end of the rainstorm. Or something like
that. Clichés are not my *fortissimo*.

To understand my juvenile psychology in the
matter you had to understand my relationship to my
father-in-law, a man of no mean bank account himself.
Since I started working for him the same day I married
his desirable (at the time) daughter, abject obeisance
has been my lot. So, I confess getting the better of a
guy megawatts brighter than Daddybucks Wemple tick-
les my sacroiliac.

Lajos was stooped, but it was more a psychologi-
cal thing than a physical one. No one played Uriah
Heep better. He sucked continually on a cigarette in a
holder, hoping, I suppose, to put one in mind of Erich
Von Stroheim. His hair and pallor were matching gray.
His build was as slight as his intellect.

He had retained his broad Hungarian accent,
and was at no apparent pains to minimize it, for, in
some circles, foreign accents were considered assets for
symphony conductors and movie moguls.

"Ah, Meester Yaytz," in his reedy tenor he must
have wished were a more mellow baritone. "Welcome.
As I told you on tah telephone, I am ready to meet
your demand. Not because I tink tey are fair by any use
of tah imagination, but because I am desperate to find
tis charlatan and to get tah return of my loved ones.

"So, evereeting is fine, no?" Lajos said, his hands
rubbing at his unctuous best. "We weel make tah deal,
yes?"

"We made the deal three time before," I said

sans tact. "But you changed the agreement after we agreed. Gazumping, they call that in the British Isles."

He spread his hands as if to say it was all beyond his control. "So, I haf had my lawyers make up tah agreement, just as you like."

"Good," I said. When he made no move to show it to me, I said, "May I see it?"

He looked hurt—as though I were doubting his word. As though he didn't realize no one's word bore *more* doubting. Reluctantly he produced the document from his middle drawer and passed it over his unkempt desk.

I could tell at first glance Lajos was up to his usual hanky-panky. He had blithely knocked ten percent off the big numbers and altered the terms of conditions of location and proof of death, should that apply.

I looked Lajos in the eye. Bluffing was another of his skills. I just stared, and I finally broke him.

"What?" he asked.

I didn't respond, but took a pen from my jacket pocket and slowly, carefully restored the contract to our last verbal agreement. I initialed all the changes and wrote "As amended" over the signature lines, and signed my space. I handed it across the desk to Lajos and watched the lines on his face contort to show me how hurt he was.

"But tees alterations was only for clarification. You know you haf no agent, so I naturally tought I would be justified in reducing your fee tah amount of tah agent's commission. In our business, we all haf agents."

"Very nice," I said. "There it is. You may take it

or leave it."

He shook his head in despair. "Why are you so hard?" he asked.

"Honoring agreements is *hard?*"

"You are unusually rigid."

"Oh? Well, let me tell you why. First, you are, as they say down at the pool hall, richer than God. I am frankly embarrassed to see you nickel and dime me when you haul in tens of millions on those juvenile pandering pictures you make. Second, you want me to go after the head hauncho of Techsci, an ersatz religion noted for cutting off at the knees anyone who looks at them cross-eyed. Maiming can be so unpleasant. Death more so. Third, you got my name from Scumbag Hadaad, my maiden voyage nemesis. He recommended me to someone else and it was nothing but trouble. I solved the case and was swindled out of my fee."

"Well, you charge so much, it is natural sometimes you lose."

"Nice of you to say so," I said. (I'd reported those two Hadaad misadventures in *The Missing Link* and *The Con*). "That was in my foolish and misguided youth. When you work contingency, you take risks. You don't always succeed. What I want to avoid is succeeding and not being paid."

"You weel be paid. We haf tah escrow."

"Which I insisted on." I was referring to the part of the agreement that stipulated the money be placed in escrow and released to me on certification of my success. Leaving payment up to the discretion of Lajos Bohem was unassisted suicide.

"So, do we haf a deal or not?"

I waved at my "amended" contract in his hands.

"Up to you," I said.

He looked at the contract, ponderously leafing through the pages and shaking his head as though I had done him wrong. "Hadaad, you know, is only acquaintance. He weel not be eenvolved in any way. He is merely a person who gave me your name."

Incredible, I thought. The man who gave me the most trouble is responsible for more referrals than anyone else.

"I weel haf it retyped," he said.

I shook my head. "Too chancy," I said. "Every time you retype you edit. This is not a movie script, it's a contract. I'm weary of the old bait and switch. Sign it now, in my presence. Initial the changes or we forget it."

He signed.

What he signed was an agreement to put into escrow the tidy sum of $250,000, payable as follows:

I would get $50,000 each on finding his wife and daughter alive. Half of that for each if they were dead and I could prove it. Another $50,000 each if I returned them to him.

The other $50,000 if they didn't return to Techsci—this he held out for a package deal. Not $25,000 each, $50,000 for both. If one went back, no payoff.

Lajos let it be known by winks and shrugs that if the leader were dead there might not be the same hold on his women, and reluctantly they should be easier to pry loose—his words.

Lajos sat back in his chair in an attitude of supreme self-satisfaction. He took a deep pull on his cigarette and smoke filtered through the ciggy holder and out his nostrils, putting me in mind of the dragon he most assuredly was.

"I haf not tole you, but I am bringing out a peecture and it is more difficult every day to get publicity. The trades haf been unfair in making me into a not nice man who drives his girls away. You bring tem back and we will put a stop to tat talk *and* get some priceless press in the bargain."

"Now," I said, "what can you tell me about Dawn and your wife? Who were their friends?"

Lajos Bohem stood with his hand on his hip, his other holding the cigarette holder to his mouth. It was stylized drama for a guy with little style. "Dawn had soo many good friends. I don't know where to start. An ideal childhood really—I was my wife's best friend. Find Dawn. Suzanne weel be with her."

There was something in his tone and that phony Eric-von-Stroheim cigarette pose that made me think he was protesting too much.

"Start with her *best* friend," I said.

"Yees—" he lit up as though I had been an inspirational muse, "—that would be Barbara Wilkins—her father's tah director. Tey haf a mansion in horse country—Barbara rides, as did Dawn. God knows what she is doing now, but I doubt it has anything to do with riding horses."

He scrawled Ms. Wilkins' address and phone number in a hand that bespoke aspirations to the medical profession.

I had a more difficult time getting pictures of his women out of him. He was intent on me carrying two publicity poses used by movie stars for identification of his lovelies—his wife's taken when she was twenty.

"Mr. Bohem—"

"Oh, Lajos, pleaze—"

"Yes—Lajos—fine. Don't you have any snapshots, informal poses—something someone *today* is liable to recognize them from?"

He frowned, he puffed, he harumphed. "What is wrong wit tees?" he asked, waving at the pictures in my hands. "Perfectly good pictures."

"Do you think wherever they are, they are looking like this? You think anyone could recognize either of them today from these glossy publicity stills?"

More puffing, more posing. "I weel look," he said at last. "Perhaps my secretary has someting."

2

Tyranny Rex was somewhere in the heartland trying to fob off her little glass figurines to the unsuspecting. I tried to tell her her two recent creations, the urinating farmboy and the defecating cow might not be hot items in the bible belt, but there was, as usual, no telling Tyranny Rex anything. All I would have to do was leave her a note and promise a phone call. Our two children, August Wemple Stark, a boy, sort of, and Felicity the girl, were more or less grown—enough to be mercifully out of the house. Our contact is kept to a minimum—their choice, but I don't fight it. I have this peculiar vision of someone telling them their father is missing, and them saying, "*Who?*"

I made a stop at the Torrance Library to start me off on Techsci. There, a slight, soft spoken gentleman guided me through the print media maze of Techsci lore. History, a manifesto, a best selling book on the "philosophy," some whacko science fiction books by the founder that apparently these books made their way to the bestseller list by dint of the groupies visiting the stores on the *New York Times* list and buying huge quantities, which were then recirculated and sent back to the stores, sometimes with the same store's own labels already on them.

There were a couple biographies of the founder, J. Kent Morgan. One by a fawning, fervent believer, another by Morgan's estranged son, reliably unfavorable.

The most helpful newspaper stuff came from a *New York Times* Sunday magazine piece by a man named Frank Crouse. The piece was around seven years old, and when I called the *New York Times* for him, I was told he had retired to Carmel, California. They said they were not at liberty to give me his phone number, but added *subrosa* he was probably listed in the phonebook—he was that kind of a guy.

Perusal of the computer catalogue listed Crouse as the author of books on a wide range of subjects—the Mormon church, Techsci, an ex-president, a movie star, a couple of spies and an axe-murderer.

Luck was with me, and the Techsci book was on the shelf. I took it to a table with selected newspaper and magazine stories. The one written by Crouse was so clear and lucid and written in a balanced way that convinced me no one could take offense.

Several pictures of J. Kent Morgan accompanied the story. He was in his sea captain getup, the captain's hat covered his balding head. From the photo I got the notion I would be looking for a portly fellow with lips like a platypus. I reasoned I could expect then an emaciated item with a full beard, toupee and possibly a nose job. He could use it. Though I didn't see how he could camouflage his hangdog eyes. If he were alive, he'd probably be living in some unexpected place—perhaps on his yacht sailing around the world, in secret, one loose lip and the ship would go KA POW!

The meat of the Crouse piece was fairly standard cult stuff. I had sharpened my incisors on a cult. In my first case, recorded in *The Missing Link,* I chased after a rich guy's daughter holed up in Berkeley, California with a group noted for selling flowers. That rich guy was the aforementioned Hadaad.

Techsci was a pop-psychology based cult, centered on ridding yourself of all your hang-ups—released, they called it—"Get released (free/purged)," was the mantra that encouraged the faithful to loosen their purse strings to the tune of over one hundred thousand clams each. Several high profile movie stars swore by the "religion," that being the operative word to avoid taxes. Crouse couldn't find much religion about it, and the cult was forever at war with the IRS to establish their bonafides. Several European countries had come down on their religious rationale and disallowed their tax-favored status. The U.S. prided itself in being broadminded about people's religious beliefs, even when the religious connections were tenuous.

Then there were the usual stories about ex-members of Techsci who accused the group of brainwashing—there was talk of threats, heavy handed tactics to silence dissidents—deprogramming. The "religion" had become a big business, and every precaution was taken to keep it that way.

I checked out *Applying Technology and Science to Everyday Living,* went home and started to read. It was deadly going, and I was adrift at understanding its success. People, I guessed, want simple nostrums for the vicissitudes of everyday life, and the fella who could give them a purchase on meaning would not go hungry. The cover said there were over seven million of these puppies in print. Of course, printing was not tantamount to selling, as in the founder's "best selling" sci-fi—but Frank Crouse seemed not to carp about it.

When my eyelids got too heavy to continue with the tome (1,150 pages of unabashed repetition) I called Carmel information to see if Frank Crouse was listed, and he was.

I called, he picked up on the second ring.

"This is Gil Yates," I said. "I'm an investigator working on a case—but, first I want you to know how impressed I am such a celebrity has a listed phone number and *answers* the phone."

He chuckled. "Thanks for the flattery," he said. "Number one, I'm not a celebrity, number two, try as I might have in my career to make enemies, I don't think I succeeded. What are you investigating?"

"Techsci and the whereabouts of J. Kent Morgan, as well as Dawn and Suzanne Bohem."

There was a long silence. "Are you there?" I asked at last.

"Hmm," he said. "Yeah. You may have hit on my one success."

"Success?"

"Yes—at making enemies."

"Techsci—?"

"Yeah."

"I read your piece, but it was so blasted fairly written I couldn't get your take on it."

"How much time do you have?"

"Lots."

"Well, I've got a room full of files if you want to look at them—"

"Great! Thanks. I'm going to try to get in Morgan's compound. What do you think my chances are?"

"Slim to none," he said. "Easier to kidnap the president," he said.

"Anybody I should talk to down south before I head up there?"

"Well, what kind of info are you looking for—you want background?"

"In your *Times* piece you mentioned a guy in San Diego who was a big booster, but didn't give his name."

"Oh, Doc Detweiler. Yeah, he's a conundrum—works in an emergency room at night, sells palms by day. Has a gillion of 'em."

"Really?" My heart stopped. "I collect palms," I said.

"He's got 'em. You want the bright side of Techsci, talk to the doc. I can give you plenty of the opposite."

We made a date for me to visit his Carmel office—in the basement of his house—giving me a couple of days to check out Doc Detweiler, and do some other work in the area before alibiing my wife and father-in-law and heading north.

3

I checked the South Bay phonebook for Techsci—should I call them stores? Outlets? Headquarters? Churches seemed a stretch. I found one up on Hawthorne Boulevard in an office building that predated the big war, when this area was on the outskirts of the bean fields.

It seemed to house a few lawyers and real estate brokers on the fringe of their respective and respectable cultures. Downstairs, in the quasi-storefront setting and announced by painted letters on the window that purported to be gold, but which seemed to have faded to mustard, was the church of Techsci.

I parked in the lot in front and was made comfortable in the realization that my heap was not out of place.

Inside I was greeted by a very presentable young woman: "Welcome to the wonderful world of Techsci," she said with a cheerful, slightly aggressive salesman's edge. I thought for a moment I was in a shoe store. You could tell that without eternal vigilance the phrase could become hackneyed, shopworn, but not on the lips of this eager young damsel. I had a quick fantasy of her falling head over heels in love with me and spilling all the church's dark secrets, but it did not seem in the deck of cards. Pretty as she was, the chemistry wasn't cooking. Could I *make* it cook? Did I want to? I expect if we had been the last two people on earth, it would have been cooking.

She was attractive in the latterly, become-pretty sense. I could picture her in high school, an awkward child with stringy long hair and coke bottle glasses, shy and wanting self-esteem. It was as though her religion—or philosophy as the case may be—had given her the courage to step out of her suffocating shell and chuck the baggy dresses and coke bottle lenses for chic but modest ensembles and contact lenses, tinted blue to be sure, and a mod, short haircut that wouldn't make her ashamed should she ever be in the company of those two high profile movie stars who claimed they owed it all to Techsci; one a closet homosexual or not, the other, not.

Little Emily Strachen from Lawrence, Kansas had combined assertiveness training and a new-fangled old-time religion with just a dollop of salesmanship in the mix.

"So this boss—what's his name?"

"J. Kent Morgan."

"Yeah—didn't he write books or something—"

"Sure did," she said, glad to be able to brag about her founder. "Bestsellers."

"Yeah?" I tried to be suitably impressed. "What kind of books?"

"Science fiction. Like he predicts what's going to happen in the future."

"Really? You read any of them?"

"Every one," she said, with a perky pride in her voice.

"Good?"

"Oh, I so enjoyed them."

That didn't precisely answer the question, but I didn't press.

"Didn't I read somewhere the founder is a recluse?"

"He's given the best years of his life to Techsci, and now—in his later years, he is choosing a simpler life. Lord knows he earned it. He turned the operation of the church over to others."

"Wasn't the IRS hounding him or something?"

"Any organization this large comes up against the IRS from time to time. We are a legitimate religion and they have finally acknowledged it." It sounded as though she were reading from a manual of instructions of what to say when the thorny questions were asked. I noticed her interest in me cool with each passing question.

"And the lawsuits? Wasn't there talk of a lot of those?"

"Who can live in America these days without being the subject of lawsuits? In this business, it's an occupational hazard."

She said business instead of religion. I wondered if the IRS would give me a break on my taxes in exchange for that tidbit.

"I guess that's true," I said nodding sympathetically. "And you're bound to have disgruntled people in any organization, aren't you?"

"You're certainly right there," she said as her

contacts caught the light just so and flashed a blue that any sky would have been proud to call its own. "Do you want to take the test?"

"Yeah," I said, noncommittally, "that is, if you think it might help me."

"I *know* it will," she said, and scurried into a small storeroom and returned in a jiffy with the Techsci psychological test. She sat me down at a table in the window so that I might advertise to all the passing world that Techsci had bagged a live one.

The test, I'm not surprised to say, was designed for the fairly bright fifth grader or a dull seventh grader. It obviously wouldn't do to eliminate that fertile segment of the populace by asking them questions they couldn't answer.

Their little "test" specialized in questions like:

Do you ever feel inferior to others?

Do you experience stress in your work?

Each question elicited the same answer from virtually everybody, and each answer made them the perfect candidate to gain release through the auspices of Techsci.

I could have written the test.

So when this became apparent to me, less than a quarter of the way through, I started answering about half of the questions wrong, just to see how old blue eyes reacted.

When I finished, I handed her the paper. "How long till I know how I did?"

"Oh, I'll correct it right now—but there's no passing or failing, it's just to see if our program would benefit you." With that she let her eyes pass over my test paper. I had doubts she was absorbing anything with that speed-reading technique. "Good," she said, when her blue-tinted contact lenses reached the bottom of the page. "You exhibit many of the qualities we are about to work on with virtually guaranteed results."

"Really?"

She nodded solemnly.

"What do I have to do next?"

"Talk to one of our counselors. I can set that up for you right now if you like."

"How much does it cost to get released?"

"It's a long and arduous process—five distinct levels."

"How long?"

"Up to you. How serious you are. How much time can you devote to your well-being—how much is it worth to you?"

"Well, it may be more a matter of how much I *can* pay."

"Believe me, many people have given us all their worldly goods and were so grateful they only wished they had more to give."

"That so?" I clucked my tongue in admiration.

"The counselor will go over the specifics—just go through that door, it's down the hall on your right. Mr. Empleman will come to greet you—and I look forward to welcoming you aboard."

Good as her word, Mr. Empleman, a bank-tellerish sort, greeted me in the inner hall, took me to a room with a long table in it, and we sat across from each other. A polished box was on the table between us. Mr. Empleman laid it all out, astonishing me in the process. The price tag on the first series of courses and analysis was barely short of my net after taxes for my toil at the niggardly feet of Daddybucks Wemple, Realtor Ass. But the good news was I could take up to five years to complete the course, at which rate I could get released in a mere twenty-five years—just in time to be an unburdened corpse. In this racket it behooved you to start young and have a trust fund. The good news was they would take a mortgage on my house as payment. I could just imagine explaining to my chesty spouse my co-mortgagee and her tight-fisted father— the lien holder.

"Before we go any further," he said, "I need to give you another psychological test." He opened the shiny wood box on the table—perhaps mahogany—and withdrew two tin cans with wires coming out of them. He handed them to me. "Here," he said, positioning the box so he could read the dial that was left inside the box after the tin cans were withdrawn. He positioned the lid so I couldn't see the dial.

He began asking innocuous questions: where was I born, was I married, what was my job? I could soon see this little ersatz lie detector could lead down forbidden paths. When he asked if I loved my wife I called a halt to the proceedings.

"Well," he said, "I can already see strong signs of inner tension that it would behoove you to release from your subconscious. Living with tension and stress is no picnic. I know—I had it—I got released from mine."

"You must have been rich," I muttered.

"No, just a working stiff. I saved what I didn't spend on tobacco and strong drink and spurious, depraved entertainment—and I got a discount for working in the office here. I'm still working some of it off after the fact, but I can tell you, whatever it costs, it is well worth it. To be released from all that garbage that clogs your systems and bogs you down—so life becomes a misery rather than the joy it is meant to be—I'm here to tell you there is just nothing like that release. I only wish I had discovered it sooner."

"Yeah," I said—"it's quite a long course—"

"But the time flies. You will tell yourself 'Why didn't I think of that?'—it's so simple—but we don't think of the obvious and the simple—we're too bogged down in our everyday miseries. We need others to monitor our shortcomings—we couldn't see them ourselves if we fell on them. We need this to set us on the right path and to keep us on the straight and narrow until we achieve full release."

"How did you hear about Techsci?"

"I read Morgan's book, *The Simple Miracle of Techsci*—I was hooked."

"Did you ever meet the boss?"

"The boss?"

"The founder?"

"No, I never did. He'd gone up north by the time I got far enough to warrant his notice."

"Could you go up north to where he is if you'd wanted to?"

"I think that is very select company. Aides he's trusted for years. Oh, I don't say it is impossible, if I harbored those aspirations, but it is not something any Tom, Dick, or Harry can achieve. I think in almost all cases you have to achieve the ultimate release to be accepted in the chief's company."

I nodded my understanding and acceptance of his wisdom.

He tried his best to close the deal. Offered me a two and a half-percent discount for signing on the spot. I demurred, told him I'd read the book first like he did and perhaps that would sell me.

"Well, okay," he said, obviously disappointed. "You can get a copy in the reception area—where you came in."

I thanked him—he escorted me back to blue eyes, giving me the feeling he was afraid I might wander into dark recesses where I was not welcome.

I bought the book. It wasn't cheap—$49.95, but as blue eyes said it was 900 pages and packed full of the most wonderful, helpful information for self-improvement that I would realize on reading it, it was worth many times that paltry amount. I didn't tell him I'd skimmed through another Techsci tome—1,150 eye-numbing pages. But, I reasoned, you could never have too much information.

I pointed my "economy" car back to my tract house, preparatory to my foray into the fields of Dawn Bohem's friends, south to Doc Detweiler and his palms, and then on north to Carmel to see what light Frank Crouse could shed on the miracle of Techsci.

4

The Wilkins place looked more like a movie set than a house. I'd called ahead, and, while there was some confusion in her voice, Barbara agreed to see me. She told me she might be on horseback because she was preparing for a national dressage competition and had not a moment to spare.

It sounded a little hoity-toity to me, but I never looked a gift horse in the teeth.

Out back behind the two story French country house manor, I found Barbara astride one lovely piece of horseflesh. I don't pretend to be a horse *aficionado* myself, but I know one when I see one. It was responding to Barbara's reins and doing some fancy footwork. I always thought it peculiar that people could get so worked up about an animal achieving with tedious practice some movement that man could make with ease.

"Oh, hi," she said on seeing me lumber toward the corral where she and the horse were fenced in with glistening milk white fences. "You're Mr. Bates?" she asked, dismounting but keeping the reins in hand, and

23

extending the other. I shook her pretty hand.

"Yes—Yates," I said, "Gil Yates."

"Oh, sure," she said. "Like *Rawhide*. I saw some of the tapes. My father directed some of them early in his career."

I couldn't tell if she were apologizing for her father. "Rowdy Yates was Clint Eastwood. I *adore* Clint Eastwood," she said. "The other one was Gil something, wasn't he?"

"Favor," I said, in admiration of her perspicacity for one so young.

"I guess Gil Yates is better than Rowdy Favor," she giggled, dismounting.

"Well," I said weakly, "when Yates is your family name, that could be a little tough."

Barbara Wilkins was a pretty thing in that polished, debutante way.

She held out her hand—"Well, whatever, I'm pleased to meet you. This is Cocoa, my horse, Mr. Yates."

I looked at the horse and wondered how I was supposed to react. "Hi, Cocoa," I said, and that seemed to fit the bill. "So, I'm told you were Dawn Bohem's best friend."

She looked at me as though I had a screw loose. "That's a bit of a stretch," she said. "That sounds like her pushy dad talking. I saw her a couple of times but there was no chemistry."

"Oh," I said, not hiding my disappointment. "Well, sorry to bother you, I guess. Know who I might talk to—who *was* her best friend?"

"Sure. Sophie Weintraub. Couldn't have been closer," she said with an edge.

"What can *you* tell me about Dawn?"

"Not much," she said, "Sophie can tell you more. They had the chemistry. I know Dawn was not nuts about her old man—but how could you be? She was a bit of a plodder—an outsider—didn't fit with the in crowd."

"That was you?"

"What?"

"The *in* crowd. You?"

"Oh," she blushed. "I don't mean that the way it sounded."

"How *do* you mean it?"

She blushed, thought a moment, then said, nodding, "I guess the way it sounds."

"Did she ever talk to you about Techsci?"

"That goofy cult?" she shook her head. "She was here one day, gone the next. I think it was a sudden thing."

The name Sophie Weintraub didn't bang any gongs with me. I looked at my list from Lajos Bohem—sure enough, Sophie Weintraub was not on it. I relayed this intelligence to Barbara.

"I'm not surprised—"

"Oh? Why not?"

"You'll see—"

"Can you tell me where to find her?"

She smiled conspiratorially. "She tends bar at the Dungeon on Melrose—in West Hollywood."

"A bartender? The *Dungeon?*"

"'Fraid so," she shrugged. "I hear it's good money."

"Ever been?"

"Oh, no," she said. Then she shot me a look of

kinship. "No chemistry," she said. But she wouldn't say anymore.

"Know her shift?"

"Sorry—no. I expect it's at night. Good luck—" and she was back on the horse, and I thought, what an effective way to terminate an interview.

"So long, Cocoa."

The Dungeon on Melrose looked pretty much like its name. It's a little difficult to describe, though the Marquis de Sade would not have been uncomfortable there. But I was. Mace, chains, mail and bludgeons were on the walls, and some Hollywood set designer had gone berserk plastering walls to look like a dungeon. The front door and restroom doors had bars on them.

At first glance, I thought I'd come at the wrong time. The bartender on this shift was a man. It took a few moments for it to hit me that there were more women than you usually find in a bar. I blamed it on the seriously subdued lighting.

The smells were musk mingled with Old Spice— a kind of artificial male pheromone fighting Rose of Sharon or Lily of the Valley or one of those female wannabe fragrances.

There were only a handful of couples at the tables—most doing some serious mooning over each other—one couple seemed to be in the throes of a spat, but nothing overly dramatic.

The music piped in from God knows where was a bumping, grinding, metallic rock. Not my era or my taste. Could I picture my daughter, Felicity, in this milieu? I could picture her almost anywhere, but this was a stretch.

I sauntered over to the bar to ask when Sophie came on. I tried to fit my saunter to the environment, like Henry VIII on his way to a spousal beheading. I'm sure I failed.

The guy behind the bar was dressed in white pants and a blue oxford cloth button-down shirt. He was dusty blond and sported an old-fashioned hair cut—the kind we had when I was in school.

"Hi," I said being sportingly jocular. "What time does Sophie come on?"

He looked at me through a cocked eye, "Who wants to know?"

I almost had to laugh at that. Somehow the toughness in the words was not matched by the timbre of the voice, the testatura was amiss. "Gil Yates," I said, extending my hand. He looked at it a moment as though checking for leprosy. Apparently I passed, because he forked his mitt over the bar and shook mine. He was smooth and delicate, and I had an instant envy of his youth.

Then he shocked the pants off me. "I'm Sophie," he said—or she said, as the case may be, and ultimately *was*.

"Oh," I said, "sorry."

She waved a hand, and smiled a wry smile. "It would be a disappointment to knock yourself out to look like a man and not be mistaken for one once in a while."

"So—good—then—so—I—mean—" I was tongue-tied—"Dawn Bohem—you know her?"

"I know her."

"I have some info you were her best friend."

She nodded, noncommittally. "What's your

interest, Mr. Yates?"

"I'm looking for her."

"Why?"

"She's missing," I said, trying to match the non-committal stare.

"No she's not. She's off with Techsci."

"Do you know where? They're all over the world."

"It's Lajos, isn't it? He's pretending he wants to find her again?"

"He wants to—yes."

She shook her head. "Stay away from Lajos—he's trouble."

"I surmised as much," I said.

"It's obvious he didn't approve of me—or of Dawn's...shall we say, predilections?"

"Oh—"

"Obviously that pretentious turd wanted a debutante, but that was not Dawn. Bet he told you Barbara Wilkins was her best friend."

I smiled at her perception.

"Didn't even mention me, did he?"

"Ah...I ah...no."

She was called away to mix some drinks. I cased the clientele again and noted that the 'men' among them were really women.

When she came back, she said, "Well, I can't help you. I don't hear from Dawn—I don't know where she is—you might say she's conflicted."

"How about you?"

"No—I know who I am. No conflicts at all."

"If I find her, would you like me to take a message from you?"

She studied me with her big blue eyes. I could see what Dawn had seen in her. Maybe it was the leprosy test again, but she sighed and said, "Tell her I love her—I can't get her out of my mind. I miss her terribly. Tell her to come home to me. Think that's trite?"

"No...I..."

"Well, maybe it is. But it's also true."

"I'll tell her," I said. "Say, if I do find her, would you meet her somewhere?"

"In a heartbeat," she said, and moved down the bar to do a daiquiri for a patron.

I never did have a good grasp on this kind of scene where females fancied females but wanted to make them men. Why not, if that were the case, just cut straight to the straight males?

Then I thought, I preferred females, why shouldn't they?

I left via the bathroom. The dungeon bar doors were open and on the regular doors were two signs—one said "Women"—the other said—"All others."

5

Getting free of my "day job" for the out-of-town phase was always a challenge. Perhaps there is something to be said for working for your father-in-law, but I don't know what it is.

I have made some delightfully large fees in this investigating game, surprising perhaps no one more than myself. So why do I put up with Elbert August Wemple, Ass. gasbag? Is it because I'm afraid I'll never get another whopping fee? Afraid I'll be out in the cold with nary two nickels to rub together? Or am I a masochist who secretly enjoys being dumped on day in and day out? Or if I wanted to be especially generous in self-appraisal, I might posit taking the guff and knowing I didn't have to was an opportunity for retribution too delicious to pass up.

In real estate, we speak of the highest and best use for a property. The old warehouse that houses that miser Elbert August Wemple and Associates saw its highest and best use as a repository for derelict machine parts. Daddybucks Wemple thought packing the old warehouse with realtor associates would raise the level of use. He was wrong.

Naturally he thought he "stole" the property, but we still haven't got all the grease off the floor, and I am just old fashioned enough to have a nagging nostalgia for windows in the work place.

Daddy Dandruff mistakenly believes that perching himself on that ridiculous platform at the front of the room—within spitting distance of yours truly—elevates his stature in the eyes of his minions. That's a laugh. He could be floating overhead on a skyhook and it wouldn't do diddly for his stature.

He'd call me up for a conference. I referred to my part in our "conferences" as sleeping with my eyes open. Daddybucks liked to hear himself talk, and responses other than "Yes, sir," were seldom called for.

When I settled in I think he was going on about a new building he'd bought in the hinterlands and how stupid the management was. But don't hold me to it.

As Dr. Seuss said, Daddybucks just keeps biggering and biggering. He has this thing about not paying income tax. If he buys enough apartments, the theory goes, he won't have to pay any. Leona Helmsley said taxes are for little people, and she wouldn't get any argument from Daddybucks.

At the first lull I interjected, "I'm thinking of going on a cycad tour."

"A what?" he asked, his mind off the subject.

"About a week or two," I said, not having any idea how much time I would need.

"This is a plant you're talking about, right?"

"Right."

"And you have them at your house—?"

"Yeah."

Then he did something that shocked me so much, if I'd had false teeth, they would have fallen on the floor. He stood up and said, "Show me."

"Now?" I asked.

"Why not? You don't seem to be doing anything productive around here."

Daddybucks was not what you'd call a frequent visitor at our house. I suspect he thought it demeaning to visit a lowly employee—the fact said employee was married to his daughter notwithstanding.

But the few times he came under some pretense or other, he showed no interest in my palms and cycads. I don't think he ever went outside.

But there we were standing among my prized cycads. And if I hadn't been so averse to physical pain, I'd have pinched myself as a reality check.

"Funniest looking palm trees I ever saw."

"They're cycads."

"Psych what?"

"Cads. Cy-cads. They're millennia old. It can take one hundred years to get three feet tall."

"Why would you have a damn fool plant like that?" he asked. "You expecting to live one hundred more years?"

"No, I..."

"I mean *look* at them—I never saw such a damn fool collection of plants. No flowers, and sharp leaves covered with stickers. You'd have to be crazy to plant something like that in your yard. I see your neighbor's just as nuts as you."

He was looking at the house next door I had secretly purchased with one of my exorbitant fees so I'd have more plant room. If Daddybucks got any inkling I owned it, he'd have a stroke on the spot, for it is a truism that Elbert A. Wemple gets his kicks keeping me down, no doubt so he can shine next to me in the eyes of his daughter, Tyranny Rex. Or, as he so charmingly saddled her, Dorcas.

Yes, I kid you not, and I think referring to her as Tyranny Rex rather than Dork is an act of charity on my part.

Daddybucks looked at the small signs I had placed under my pride and joys and mangled the pronunciations En-cef-ahLAR-tos became In-syphilis-artoss. Trispinosis (*Try*-spin-oh sis) became Tris PINE uhses. But he was trying—that's what astonished me. *Worried* me, actually. Was he going to take an interest in cycads and suggest he accompany me on my bogus tour?

Then, just when I thought I could never be surprised again, Daddybucks invited me to lunch. I must have stammered something terrible because he sank to draconian measures—he patted me on the shoulder as though I needed encouragement and that would do it. Both preposterous assumptions.

All the way to the restaurant—a greasy spoon on Crenshaw that he actually thought was good—a proposition you could only subscribe to if someone had taken a blowtorch to your taste buds—I quietly agonized over what he wanted from me. I had nothing to give, and he surely knew that. It crossed my mind that he was just suddenly being friendly but the thought evaporated as quickly as it occurred.

We sat down at the bare plank table which had been faithfully shellacked until the proprietor gave it up as a futile gesture for his clientele, whom he finally adjudged not able to tell the difference.

"Best hamburger in town," Daddybucks said, and promptly ordered a doubly patty version—"Make it two," he said with a sidelong glance in my direction where, if he'd had the slightest perception, he would have seen my dismay. What he saw instead was my inability to contradict him.

Hamburger, ground beef to the gourmets, is graded by fat content, with twenty-five percent fat being considered heart attack fodder. The lower the fat content, the holier the consumer. This establishment, which I don't dare name, is noted for burgers with reversed ratios—so if you get twenty-five percent meat, a mistake has been made in the kitchen.

The burgers came accompanied by a pile of fries that the grease had irreversibly permeated, leaving them a soggy mess. The burger bun was so saturated in fat it was wet to the touch.

Daddybucks sank his falsies into the soggy mess and groaned with pleasure. I got nauseous just watching him. I didn't dare look down at my plate for fear I might throw up just at the prospect of putting it in my stomach. My employer slash father-in-law, was so transported with the fare he didn't seem to notice I wasn't eating, I kept a glass of water in hand as a less than brilliant stroke of deception.

"I'm on to you, Malvin," he said. Malvin Stark is my real name. Gil Yates is make-believe. But the thought that Elbert A. Wemple, Ass. knew about my secret private investigating racket, put me way off my feed—in this case, mercifully.

"What do you mean?" I asked meekly. I was too darn meek in the presence of this blowhard.

34

"I know what you're up to," he said, his jaws chomping his greaseburger as though the action was a stimulus to his insight.

"Up to?"

"Yeah. This fantasy about going on cycad conferences—jeez, you even took a cruise to one—ho ho," he said, winking at me. He was referring to a case I had chronicled in *Bluebeard's Last Stand.* Fortunately Daddybucks doesn't read. Oh, not that he can't—television is just so much easier.

I had to catch myself from blurting incriminations in misguided defense. After all, he could have his suspicions—he would not be Elbert A. Wemple, you-know-what without his omnipresent suspicions—and just be fishing for a lead. I didn't give it to him, and I'd resolved to slowly deny any guess that came close to reality with a guffaw. After all, T. Rex, his very daughter and my very wife—*very*—was told I was investigating a murder (in my slim volume, *What Now, King Lear?*) and she had guffawed at the ridiculousness of the notion. Of course, I would not be astonished to discover Daddybucks had a touch more perspicacity than his dorky daughter.

I held my ground. "I'm afraid I really don't know what I'm up to. I hope it's something good."

"Yeah—good! That's a good one. Good all right." He'd completed his burger and reached across the table, took mine and absent-mindedly started greasing his dentures with it as though it were the most natural thing in the world.

Then it was as though the grease loosened his tongue, and he leaned forward like an oleaginous TV interviewer. "No good denying it—I know you got babes."

"Babes?" It didn't register at first—so surprised was I; then I remembered he'd accused me of that before, but it was just one of his passing denigrations, to which I'd become so accustomed.

"Babes—you got it."

"Well, I..."

"No, don't deny it. I'm not so stupid I don't see those ridiculous plants for what they are."

"What are they?"

He nodded, the burger grease coursing down his dewlaps. "A front. A blind for the babes. It's only common horse sense. What guy in his right red-blooded mind would be interested in those silly-assed plants when he could be spending his time with a gorgeous girl?"

"Me?" I said, wanting it to sound like an affirmative statement rather than the half question that came out.

"And butterflies give milk," he smirked. "No," he shook his head, "you can't put that one over on old Wemple—he wasn't born yesterday, you know."

"Really—sir—your daughter is the only woman in my life."

"'s okay," he said, waving his grease soaked fingers at me before dipping them into my French fries, "the same woman can be a drag after a while. But tell me something"—he was leaning again—in for the kill, "you got only one—or a whole bushel of 'em?"—clearly his hope was with the second alternative.

"Your imagination is better than the reality," I said elusively.

"Tell that to the marines," he said, polishing off the last of my lunch. "But hey, more power to you, my lad. Take all the time you want—sow the oats. And," he said, winking at me, "if you have a surplus I wouldn't be opposed to taking one or two of them off your hands, should that be to your benefit."

Crazy old coot. What could I say? "I'll keep you in mind," I said, trying to visualize the woman who could find any socially redeeming qualities in the old dandruff bag. He may be gauche, I thought, but at least he's rich and can treat me to this gourmet lunch.

"Oh, by the way," he said, patting the breast pocket of his jacket, trying to project surprise—"get the check, will you? I seem to have forgotten my wallet."

6

Bright sun cleared my way to Fallbrook, north of San Diego.

I'd called ahead to make sure Doc Detweiler would be on site for my first visit. It was when he said, "What are you looking for," that I formulated my plan. Be a palm and cycad buyer (who better?) and approach Techsci only obliquely.

"Oh," I said—"anything and everything—preferably unusual."

Down in Fallbrook, there are cities of greenhouses stretched across the land like beached whales. They provide the vehicles to fill our needs for beauty—and on a lesser scale, nutrition.

There were so many palm trees in huge boxes on the lot before the greenhouse, that there was hardly any place to park. Luckily my car was small—it is hard to imagine a car smaller.

I went into the greenhouse and my first thought was, if green plants were our only source of oxygen, was it possible to suffocate on oxygen? There were so many palms and cycads of all sizes crammed into the cavernous greenhouse, I didn't see how any human had a chance to survive.

Greenhouses were an enigma to me. You had all this glass to let light in, then whitewashed it so you didn't get too much light—you wanted heat, but not too much, so an elaborate overhead fan system was installed.

Doc was an endomorph and an A personality at the same time—chain-smoking, working at night in an emergency room, ministering to the sick and broken among us, and by day plying his trade in his greenhouses and open fields. His walk down the aisles of cycads and palms was a modified waddle with a side sidling crablike motion, and intermittently he would tug up his pants which had slipped their moorings. He was an overstuffed chair with sagging slip covers.

But with all those palms and cycads I was in heaven. They were stuffed in the two greenhouses like pregnant sardines, and people a lot more slender than the doc couldn't walk through the aisles without being continually brushed by the leaves of the plants. To some palm lovers, this was a sensual experience. After going down my first aisle I felt as though I had gone through a dry car wash. But I was euphoric. I'd never seen so many palms and cycads in one place. Two acres under glass! Holding about ten acres of plants.

My mind fell from the case as easily as the ash of the doc's cigarette.

I was in tall grass—or clover was under my feet—however that cliché goes. I couldn't imagine duplicating the experience anywhere in the world. Heaven!

The doc was like a clothing salesman who tells you everything looks wonderful on you. Every plant had something to recommend it. I thought I had a pretty good collection until I saw this. I couldn't stop picking plants out—he had an underling cart them out front. I got a bunch of *Coccothrinax*, which the doc characterized as "cute." I got a *Wodyetia/Vetchia* cross and an *Encephalatos Dyeranius* which I had been in search of for four years. A gorgeous *Loxococcus*, a couple of unnamed species of *Macrozamia*—and that was just the beginning.

In an effort to be sociable the doc asked—"Does your wife like palms and cycads?"

I laughed. "Hardly," I said. "My wife is screwed up. She doesn't like my palms—hates my cycads. I'd get her a psychiatrist but I can't afford it. You're a doctor—got any suggestions?"

He looked at me kind of funny-like. "Yeah," he said, "I got some ideas. Come on in here—follow me—" and he led me to a temporary portable building, unlocked the door and went in before me.

Inside there was a conference table that virtually filled the room, a gray carpet on the floor and prints of palm trees on every wall.

"Sit down," he said, and we sat across the table from each other. "Now about your wife," he said, "you might think this is a peculiar question, coming from a doctor, but is she religious at all?"

"God no," I snorted.

He nodded as though he already had the inside track on Tyranny's psyche. "Is she receptive to new ideas?"

I laughed again. "Tyranny?"

"Tyranny? That's her name?"

"Tyranny Rex. Nickname," I said. "Her real name is worse: Dorcas."

His raised eyebrows did not connote disagreement. "Do you call her that...when you're with her? Tyranny Rex? To her face?" he added, as though I might have missed the point.

I shook my head. "You think I have a death wish?"

He smiled. I didn't get the impression he was a big laugher. "She have self-doubts?"

I was on the spot. How far could I take this? I knew he wanted me to say Tyranny was plagued with self-doubts, but I didn't know anyone with less self-doubt than Tyranny Rex.

"That's a safe bet," I said.

"Mind muddled—sometimes to the point of inactivity?"

'You could say so," I said.

"Well, I was similarly afflicted."

"You?" I said astonished.

"Yes, me," he said. "A doctor, you're going to say next. We're just people like everyone else—with specialized training. So I came upon this scientific religion—a psychology for those in trouble—and who isn't?"

"What kind of trouble?"

"Self-doubt, paralyzed into inactivity—searching for meaning, a clear conscience, that kind of thing. Anyway, this religion is based on release—release from worry, from tension, from self-doubt."

"Sounds good. How's it done?"

"You take courses with the goal of getting this release."

"Nirvana, sort of?"

"Call it what you want, but it's a feeling, when you achieve it, like no other."

"You've achieved it?"

He nodded solemnly as though I'd paid him the highest compliment and he was accepting modestly his due. "Have you heard of Techsci?"

I cocked my head as if to jog my memory. "Sounds familiar," I said.

"Did *me* a world of good, I can tell you. I'm a new man."

The way he ran around like a decapitated chicken, I wondered what he was like before he achieved peace through release.

"Anyway, if you're interested I can put you in touch with people who can get you started."

"Me? I thought...my wife..."

"Oh, sure—her too. But I can tell you might benefit from it."

"Me? How so?"

"Oh, I can tell, you're a guy who's anal—the way you look at the plants and watch your pennies."

That shocked me. See yourself as others see you. I don't know how he got that idea. I never complained about a price or asked him to take less. I think it was a sales ploy: put me on the defensive so I never questioned anything.

"Any drawbacks to this Techsci?" I asked.

"Nah," he said. "Oh, you'll always have complainers. You read in the papers about the disenchanted few when ninety-nine and forty-four one-hundredth percent are delighted."

"Yeah, I seem to remember something about brainwashing."

"Wow," he laughed. "Yeah, that's right. That's the whole idea—wash your brain clear of all the nonsense."

"Oh," I said, like a dummy, "I thought they

were talking about brainwashing to keep them paying—"

He waved a dismissive hand—"Always going to have a few malcontents."

He took a prescription pad from his pocket and scribbled a name and phone number on it. He pushed it across the table to me and I glanced at it. Totally unreadable. I looked up at the doc. He was oblivious.

Just as well, I wasn't going to send Tyranny in any case. She'd just laugh me out of the house, and rightly so. What she needed was a concerted course to instill a scintilla of modesty in her overbearing bones.

"Well," I said, "I guess I better see what the damages are—"

"*See?*" he said pointing a finger at me.

"See what?"

You called your bill damages. Nothing damaging about it—it's a fair exchange—my plants, your money. Everybody wins."

"Is that the Techsci attitude?"

"You might say so—"

We went back outside where he sat at a small, cheap table and toted up the damages dammit. And they were substantial. So substantial that when he looked at my car and the size of the plants I'd thoughtlessly bought, he decided to throw in the delivery—I told him I was going out of town and asked him to hold them until I called.

His parting words were, "Remember, Techsci—get released."

7

I flew to Monterey, rented a car and eased on down to Carmel, which belonged to the pantheon of cutesy California tourist towns, along with La Jolla and Santa Barbara. But I think in Carmel you were more aware of the tourists. It seemed as if everyone on the circumscribed main street was a tourist, and the architecture of the dollhouse school lent itself to the attraction of those sojourners who would not be obliged to spend too much time contemplating the surreal cutes.

Frank Crouse lived only a few blocks from the hubbub and one block up from the ocean in a house that could have been used in any self-respecting production of *Hansel and Gretel.* I have been, in my time, partial to gingerbread, and beholding the Crouse house, I could taste it. Mmm good.

There was a vintage racing green Jaguar in the driveway.

My curved knuckles had barely touched the door of his house when Frank Crouse opened it, as though he were so solicitous of my welfare he didn't want me to have to wait outside a moment longer than necessary.

Crouse was a man well-weathered—who had weathered well. No over-eater, he was built just right. His eyes were covered with thick glass lenses and showed a lifetime of reading, writing, then reading what he had written.

"Nice-looking car," I said, tossing my head in the direction of the jag.

"Oh," he said, as though surprised the car was there and I had noticed it. "I'm a small-time car buff—collect a few. Had a gull wing Mercedes but the Techsci enforcers blew it up—"

"No!"

"Afraid so. Come in and sit down," he said. While I followed him in, he said, "They play for keeps."

I'd had my car blown up in a saga I recorded in *Ship Shapely*, and I wasn't eager to repeat the experience.

"What are they afraid of?" I asked, sitting on the comfortable couch—he sat in a wiry chair facing me.

"Being exposed. The thing is a scam."

"Apparently hundreds of thousands don't think so."

"People believe what they want to believe. And I don't doubt many think they are helped by Techsci."

"As some are helped by crossing the street in the rain and seeing a rainbow?"

"Whatever—but the difficulty comes when someone becomes disenchanted, and wants out. That's when the extreme paranoia sets in. Their reaction is what raises a scepter of suspicion. *If* they had nothing to hide why would they react as they do—blowing up cars, crippling people?"

"Crippling—literally—like the Mafia?"

"Not an improbable analogy," he said.

His wife came in from the kitchen. She was petite, eager to please and showed eyes of accommodation. If there was any dissention in this household, it was invisible.

The Crouse's living room was like a museum, with each object d'art perfectly displayed and nothing a half inch out of place. Rebecca Crouse had a quaint collection of porcelain figurines which put me in mind of the product of Tyranny Rex, the glass blower—only these figurines were more sublime and refined. No urinating farm boys or defecating cows.

Rebecca offered coffee, tea or orange juice. I took the latter. Frank asked me a lot of tactful questions about my trip and my work, and was so solicitous I felt like a cad to have to deceive him about my true identity—so I made it up as I went along.

From the kitchen I heard the whirring of an orange juice squeezer, making me a bit chagrined that I asked for such a labor intensive drink.

Crouse was a gentleman, not the sort of hard hitting testosterone reporter I visualized—the kind that would grab you by your shirt collar and shout, "Listen here, I want the truth or you'll be sorry." The hard drinking, cigar smoking guy who dropped his "g's". Crouse was educated, cultured and refined. His living room had a wall devoted to books that don't make the bestseller lists.

His wife smiled cheerfully when she brought the orange juice; you'd think I had done her a favor asking for it.

When I finished the orange juice, Frank invited me down to his "war room." He led me down a short hallway to a door to the outside—between two story-book bedrooms. I followed him down the outside stairs into a basement room.

The war room was small, and I suppose the litter gave it a cozy feeling—for there were papers everywhere making me wonder what good the computer setup on his desk was. There were file cabinets on the wall perpendicular to his desk—an old fashioned wooden slatted barrel chair and what looked like a leftover card table chair for me.

From the top drawer of the gray steel file cabinet he withdrew two folders of the type with elastic bands holding down the flap and in the contents. He undid the elastic with a snap.

"Fascinating guy, this J. Kent Morgan."

"What's the J for?"

"Jaime—he thought it was too androgynous. He likes the harder sounds, Kent Morgan. Jaime Morgan didn't cut it for him. Then too, I found out they taunted him in school with Hymie and that raised his anti-Semitic ire."

"Did you get to meet Morgan?"

"Oh no. By the time I did the piece he was a confirmed recluse. Oh, I tried—wrote, telephoned, even showed up at the compound. Never got any response—never got past the gate."

"But isn't it two-hundred acres or something? Surely that's not all fenced."

"No, but the living area is. Ten-foot chain link topped with razor wire. And patrolled twenty-four hours a day."

"Really? All night long?"

"Really."

"Must cost a bundle."

"Cost is no object. You can't count the millions Techsci takes in. Part of their problem is the skimming. You can't have a legitimate religion where someone is getting an inordinate amount of money. Not Kosher. Raises the hackles of the IRS. If this *were* ever taxed, I suspect it would cost them hundreds of millions of dollars—and you can bet this money has long ago disappeared."

"What are the boss's weaknesses? If I showed up with a big breasted twenty year old might I get in?"

He laughed. "'Fraid not—he's beyond that. In fact, he seems to be beyond everything. Rumor has it he is just an old alcoholic being propped up by competing factions until they can sort out who will run the show after he's gone. It is not a fight he discourages—probably because he sees it as life insurance: As long as he can keep them guessing who he will designate in his will as his successor, he can keep them off balance—just uncertain enough to keep them from killing him."

"Who are the factions?"

"The main contenders are the aptly named Terrance Savage—he's running the show now—and Vic Neeley, who is his constant companion and has been for almost ten years. All the time he was in hiding. Horace Bernheimer is his lawyer and must figure in any resolution because he writes the wills and codicils."

"Know what the last will says?"

He shook his head—"Nobody does. That's how

he keeps them dancing."

"Seems to me the factions would be currying the favor of the lawyer."

"I'm sure they are. Oh, the uses and abuses of power are endlessly fascinating. Helped make Shakespeare so popular."

"So who would it be useful for me to talk to? Anybody that could get me into the man himself—or someone who could point me to the women I'm looking for?"

"Well," he said, "start with Morgan's wife, Belinda. If you could loosen her up, you might get an earful."

"How so?"

"She served time for him—took the rap on a stupid Watergate-like break-in of the FBI. When she got out of jail, Morgan would have nothing to do with her." He copied her address and phone number from his file to a list he was making for me—from the same pen he wrote another name—"Then there's the son—Phil Ramsey, couldn't stand his father—changed his name. Pop disowned him—I'm sure he's written out of the will."

While Crouse was flipping pages and writing more names down for me, I asked, "What would happen if I just bust through the gates and found him?"

"They'd probably throw a net on you."

"But if I did get through, what would I find?"

"Oh, perhaps the classic story of decline. A man once powerful and resourceful at loose ends—gone to seed. Mental processes dubious. I think he's lost his grip and the mice around the king rat are scurrying for control."

"Who will get it?"

"Good question. I'm tempted to say the most cunning sycophant of the bunch, but that doesn't credit the old captain with any cunning of his own."

"Which he hasn't lost?"

"Some things we don't lose. I suspect cunning is one of them."

"Is there some approach that might do the trick? Something that would appeal to him?"

"Well, I'd say flatter his vanity, but I expect he'd see through it. Besides, you'd have to get *to* him first, and his guards won't let you." He shook his head. "No, I can't think of anything."

"What were his interests?"

"Power. Ego. He created this outlandish autobiography of himself where he'd been everywhere, done everything. He liked the sea—it was a good place to hide. When he began this hideout routine, he took his most trusted aids on his yacht and they sailed up and down the seven seas, out of reach of the long arms of the IRS and process servers. If he hadn't, he might have spent the rest of his life in court."

"I talked to two Techsci reps in Torrance, and Doc Detweiler. Any other friends I should seek out?"

He laughed. "Enemies are easier. All his friends are in the compound with him."

"But why would he take a young girl—if you say he's beyond amorousness?"

"Oh, he loves young girls. His disciples, he calls them. They are glorified servants."

Back upstairs I demurred at the gracious dinner invitation, saying I'd better move on to my first stop. I thanked them both profusely, and though they said the pleasure had been theirs as many people do automatically, the Crouse's made it sound as if they really meant it.

Frank Crouse's parting words to me were, "Call me if I can be of any help—and keep your back to the wall."

8

It was a pleasant drive from Carmel to San Jose, where I hoped to smoke out Belinda Morgan.

I decided not to call first, but use the bludgeon approach—just show up at the door. It was so easy to say "No" on the telephone, and besides, I looked like a Fuller Brush man—so unthreatening, it often worked.

Belinda's digs showed there was not a lot of spousal support coming her way. She lived over a garage on a busy street with a generous helping of street noise.

I needn't have worried about her willingness to talk to me. In her predicament, listeners were in short supply.

There was a hesitation in her opening the door, but when she did, the low sun hit her just so—highlighting her features like an afternoon soap opera. She looked something like a benign witch, with long stringy hair, made black in the service of eternal youth. Her smile was teenage: flashing and self-conscious—yet wary of a world that had treated her cruelly.

Belinda Morgan seemed a little disappointed when I stated my business. Perhaps she was hoping for a Fuller Brush man.

"I have a man whose daughter, then his wife, were enticed away from him and he wants them back."

"Oh, yes," she said, giving in to the weight of the world on her shoulders—"there are a lot of those. Well, I know I can't help you, but you can come in if you want."

She led me into a room compatible with the garage beneath it. "Pardon the place," she said. "I know it's not much, but it beats jail, I can tell you."

It was one room with an alcove off to the side with one of those under-the-counter refrigerators and a hot plate. As I followed her, I noticed she had maintained an enviable body. Difficult to overeat in jail, I suppose.

She turned and said, "Have a seat," waving to a rocking chair with an old, worn plaid blanket thrown over it to hide the worn out seat upholstery. She sat on her bed, which had throw pillows on it in an effort to pass it off as a couch.

"Can you tell me why you were in jail?" I asked.

She shook her head, but it was at the memory, not in denial of my request.

"Quite a few of us thought we were set up. I mean, the whole concept boggles the mind. Only eight years after Watergate it looked like we were attempting something only on a much larger scale—the IRS! The FBI! Is there any way we wouldn't be caught?"

"What were you looking for?"

"Their files," she said, as though I were a dimwit. "What they had on us."

"Where was Kent?"

"Nowhere in sight, I can tell you. Call him anything but don't call him stupid. But he got a bunch of people he was on the outs with taken care of for six years."

"Including you?"

"Especially me. I'm his fourth wife, you know— nineteen years younger. He kept getting older but his wives didn't."

"When was the last time you saw him?"

"The final pep talk for our 'mission.' I tried to see him when I got out, but he refused. I was almost fifty then after all, and he'd never had a wife that old." She sighed. "Well," she said, waving her arm across the room, "you can't say he isn't keeping me in the style he'd like me to become accustomed to."

I glanced around. It didn't take long. "Maybe he's on hard times," I offered.

She gave what was more a grunt than a laugh. "Richer than God—isn't that how they put it?"

"What's he saving it for?"

"He was a man riding high for over thirty years—making millions and salting them away."

"Switzerland?"

She nodded—"And the Cayman Islands—wherever he could hide it."

"What did he spend it on?"

"That's just it," she said, twirling her hair like a teenager, "he didn't have the knack or imagination for spending, I've come to think of making and spending money as two separate and finally incompatible arts. But he tries—oh, how he tries—to be a flamboyant spender under the pretense of getting it right, where it only serves to make people tear their hair out."

"What was your place in the organization?"

"Oh, I was an early follower. Gaga, you might say, over the leader. He was so ambitious, and that appealed to me. He made me see stars—the sky was the limit, he said. I waited my turn—patiently, obediently, through two other wives—his second and third. You'd think that should have told me something." She shook her head. "There's that wonderful Pennsylvania Dutch saying, 'We get too soon old and too late smart.' That's me."

"You paid all that money? Did you get released?"

She laughed out loud at that. "I just got released—from jail—it's the best release there is. But yes, I went the distance. He let me know subtly he wouldn't marry me if I didn't."

"Where did you get the money?"

"I worked, I saved, I put it all into Techsci. I was devolved."

"What was it like being married to the great man?"

"Tedious," she said. "His ego was in constant need of feeding. I knew it all along and I was happy to feed it, but so little was coming back to me it became a chore. That's why he has all those pretty young girls, waiting on him hand and foot. That's what he wanted all along—servant girls. He has no concept of what a wife is. Maybe that explains why there were four of us...so far!"

"You sound a little bitter?"

"Kent always said 'Hell hath no fury like a woman scorned,' and I was scorned all right—big time. So I guess I'm entitled to a little fury."

"Can you suggest any way I could get to these

women who might be in his compound?" I showed her the pictures of Bohem's wife and daughter. If she recognized them, I couldn't see it in her eyes.

"The people who know where they are, are probably in the compound outside Santa Ynez," she said. "If you can get into the compound you are a better man than I—I couldn't."

"Why is he so guarded?"

"Paranoia—most of it well-founded. Everyone is after him—the IRS, FBI, CIA. He thinks so, anyway. I can tell you, the feds were none too happy to have to settle for me in the slammer, while the big cheese was sailing the seven seas avoiding service and arrest."

"Isn't there something that would entice Kent Morgan if not out of hiding, at least to talk to me?"

"Alleviate his fears? Got a magic wand?"

"Why do you suppose the feds don't snatch him up now? It's no secret where he is—"

"I wouldn't say it is generally known—but the feds surely know—yet—"

"What?"

"Maybe the feds don't know. Maybe you or I should tell them. Probably have other things on their minds. But I think the real reason they haven't snatched him is the statute of limitations has run out."

"Any other ideas on getting in?"

"Drop out of an airplane?" she said facetiously.

"I'm not much of a flyer," I offered lamely. "Don't you know anyone inside his compound, who still thinks well of you—someone who might help?"

"Not offhand. Kent is a guy who demands abject loyalty. If he suspects you don't have it, out you go—but once out, he becomes paranoid you are going

56

to bring the organization down."

"Anyone try to do it?"

"*Anyone?*" she said startled at the question. "*Everyone.* They're all over the place."

"How do you account for the extremes—the loyalists on one hand and the disgruntled ex-Techscis on the other?"

"Don't know—except that's the sort of thing Kent inspires love—or…hate. But now I fear he is fading, is a shadow of his former self. Disguises his appearance, getting forgetful. Alzheimer's? Maybe—wanders around in his trailer."

"He lives in a *trailer?*"

"While he's building his mansion—only he can't make up his mind about anything, so the mansion withers on the vine."

"But how does he *hold* these people if he's so erratic?"

"Fear. No one is better at instilling fear in the hearts of his fellow man," she said. "Then there are the factions—each hoping to inherit the kingdom."

"Could I work them against each other?"

"If you could get to them—not that they need any help on that score. There's plenty of friction without outside help. Kent likes to play people off against each other—it makes him feel powerful."

"Wasn't there a son?"

"You mean Junior? They don't speak. A real serious mutual dislike."

"Can you tell me where to find him?"

"He just dropped out. Nobody's seen or heard from him in years. He's probably dead."

I thanked her and said goodbye, looking her in

the eye and divining that she wanted a hug. I gave it to her and I could feel her gratitude. She didn't want to let go, but seemed finally to sense a futility in the gesture.

She released me and said, "Good luck. I'm afraid you're going to need it."

9

It was an older couple—perhaps late sixties, early seventies who hosted the gathering of Techsci dropouts. Emma and Bill Ashbrook lived in a modest apartment and bore about them an air of dignity. I could tell a few minutes after meeting them it was a struggle to maintain that air.

Frank Crouse had told me about these groups and how Techsci made every effort to infiltrate the groups with an eye toward intimidation—to prevent lawsuits to regain their life's goods which they had signed over to the "church."

On Crouse's suggestions I had called ahead, and Emma Ashbrook, ever gracious, agreed I should keep the profile low. She said she knew most of the attendees at their meetings were legitimate ex-members of Techsci, but occasionally one or two strangers would wander in, putting a damper on the proceedings.

She said she would only acknowledge my presence if she knew all the attendees to be bonafides. The group was meeting to plan strategy for a lawsuit and always had to expect the presence of Techsci spies.

Emma did not know Dawn or Suzanne Bohem, but offered to ask those she could trust.

There were nine of us in their modest living room. Emma's husband Bill called the meeting to order.

"Welcome," Bill Ashbrook said to the assembled long faces. "I'm going to tell you our story. Many of you have heard it. But we find we get some relief in the telling and invite you to do the same." He paused, and it seemed as though his past was parading across his line of vision before he spoke again.

"Emma and I worked hard all our lives. She was a high school history teacher, I was a family dentist. We lived frugally, saved enough to buy a modest house, which over the years became worth almost a half a million dollars. Not in our wildest imagination did we ever foresee such a thing. That was the crux of our problem—our economic sense was out to lunch. We did our work, brought our money to the bank, and spent very little of it on ourselves. We had no children, but we were comfortable with each other. A little past midlife, I don't know exactly how it began, we started to wonder about the meaning of our existence. The idea that we were superfluous people hit us both at virtually the same time. Who would miss us if we were gone? Someone else would slide into Emma's history class effortlessly, and the students—if it's not a stretch to call that unruly mob 'students'—wouldn't know the difference. There are dentists aplenty roaming this earth. Someone else would fill the teeth and cap them with crowns. So what were our lives worth to mankind in the harsh light of day? Our estimation was not high.

"We saw a note in the paper about a self-help

fair, with over one hundred booths representing pop-psychology to, ostensibly, deep thinkers, to motivation-al gambits. It was a lark, something for an old couple to do to pass a Saturday.

"With that many booths, it's easy to go on over-load.

"I can't remember most of them—but one stood out. It was the size of four regular booths and no expense seemed to have been spared to make it glitzy. Helium spaceships floated above. Young nubiles in shiny, tight-fitting silver getups—revealing without being revealing, if you get when I mean."

There was a murmur in the room. Bill smiled.

"A young woman noticed us and came over. She wasn't pushy—she just started asking us questions, and I guess we were so flattered by the attention we answered. I asked what this was all about and she told us. It sounded ideal. There was study involved—self-improvement, a clearing of extraneous meddlesome annoyances from our subconscious. There were testi-monies from movie stars, doctors, lawyers, shoe sales-men and chambermaids. We were intrigued. We signed on the spot and made an appointment to get tested at the local outlet—I don't think they'd like to hear me call it an outlet like a store that sold Ralph Lauren sec-onds, but that's what comes to mind.

"Well, we held the tin cans as you all have, and answered some embarrassing questions under the guise of clearing our consciousness and releasing us from the terror of our hearts and minds—our bodies and souls. We got a kick out of it and wanted to go on—to see what else was in store. We told ourselves we felt better already.

"In the beginning we were delighted with the Techsci program. For the first time in our lives we felt truly positive about life and our purpose on the planet. We were happy to pay whatever we had to to get us out of life's doldrums. But after we started to see how much we could control our own lives, we wondered why we should still have to pay through the nose for the many stages of Techsci. Our questions were shot down. It was obvious questioning was not permitted and we soon became afraid of our own thoughts. We had to get out and that's when the real trouble started. We paid a huge price for what we thought only Techsci could give us.

"Then they got to the money part. They must have an inborn sense of when to go for the jugular, and we were ripe! I still remember the room with the tin cans between us and the counselor with the studious face and the slight tic in his left cheek.

"You look at someone and they don't look quite right to you—not trustworthy, but you want to believe the best of people and so you go along with it. But when he told us getting released—which we had sort of relished as a distant goal—would cost us over one hundred thousand each—we were both deflated. I mean, you could *hear* the breath leak right out of us. I had to confess right then and there that we just didn't have that kind of money and we'd had no idea. I mean, we could have gone through four years of college for that.

"'Exactly!' the man said. 'And we like to think of this program for release as a college course. It doesn't have to be paid all at once,' he said, 'and you might want to look into donating your house to the church. It's a tax deduction too.'

"You know the rest," he said, waving his arm around the apartment living room. "We'd planned on leisurely retirement, but we're still at it—tooth and nail—and it's a struggle just to keep our head above water.

"So tonight we're going to talk about our legal remedies. We aren't the first and there have been some successes, and a lot of failures. So it's not a sure thing, by any means. There are a lot of others who think like we do. Still others have been successfully intimidated by the thugs who are fueled by the most horrendous paranoia I've ever seen."

The others told similar tales. Then the meeting settled down to discussion of legal strategy, the interview of possible lawyers who would take the case on a contingency basis.

Then I was introduced—apparently Emma felt secure in her audience. They were sympathetic when I told them I was looking for a young girl to get her *released* in the old fashioned sense of the term.

Unhappily, no one had heard of her or her mother, and studying their photographs didn't jog any memories.

When the meeting adjourned, I thanked my host and hostess and passed out cards with my phone number, in case a miracle happened and one of them ran into Dawn or Suzanne, or remembered something.

The apartment was on the second floor of the medium-sized complex, and as we descended the stairs, I noticed a guy hiding in the bushes with a camera. It was pointed at us. I think I was able to avert my face before the flash went off.

"Get him!" I yelled, and the men took off after

him—but he was too fast for us—and he dove into a car at the curb and burned rubber just as we made it to the sidewalk.

"These people are uncanny," one of the men said. "They know everything."

"Well," one of the women said, "at least he didn't get into the meeting."

"Far as we know," her husband said. "Could have had the place bugged."

We said goodbye and went off in different directions—each to his own particular darkness.

10

On a whim I called my voicemail and was surprised to have a message from one of the attendees at
the Ashbrook's soiree.

Her name was Frieda Fuller—"That was quick,"
she said when I called her postal haste. "I didn't want
to say anything. We're just as paranoid as Techsci is—
bugging, infiltrating, traitors—but I have a hunch, and
it's a hunch only, that your young woman is a cadet for
the big man himself at the headquarter compound outside Santa Ynez."

"Wow—thanks a million—any idea how I could
check that?"

"No one who knows will tell you. Sorry, I can't
help you with that part of it."

"Think I could get into the compound?"

There followed a pause, then a dry chuckle. "If
you do, you won't come out alive."

"That bad?"

"Worse. Good luck. Oh, and don't tell them I
sent you."

"Check—"

"In fact don't mention my name. Since I left Techsci, I've found life is worth living again."

In the morning I left my motel fifty-nine dollars and ninety-five cents (plus tax, of course) and took my rental car back and hopped the shuttle bus for the airport. I flew to Santa Barbara, rented another car and drove up the coast and inland to Santa Ynez.

The Santa Ynez business district is almost an oxymoron. A main street that takes you to Los Olivos one way and Solvang the other, attended by a handful of side streets. Businesses are sparse. I made the rounds with my pictures and the shopkeepers seemed reserved. I couldn't tell if it was from fear of reprisal or genuine ignorance of the matter, but most of those I talked to pled ignorance. One or two had heard rumors of a religious cult but they hadn't paid much attention. It didn't affect them one way or the other. They looked pensively at my pictures and shook their heads.

I couldn't get anyone to acknowledge large purchases, until I found the grocery store. The clerk was young and on the heavy side. I suspected she had a heart of titanium, and might not be adverse to a chat.

I showed her the pictures—she rejected Suzanne out of hand—but she looked a little too long at Dawn, and I read recognition on her brow. But she shook her head with a doleful air. "Sorry, I don't know her."

"But you recognize her, don't you?"

"I don't…think so…I see a lot of people in here. Maybe some look something like that, but I couldn't swear to it."

"But if she bought a lot of stuff—would that help you recognize her—or anyone?"

"Sorry, Mister," she said. "I can't help you."

"Ever hear of Techsci?"

"I don't know. I hear a lot of stuff—don't pay attention to most of it."

I expect that was an honest statement, as she looked like a damsel with a capacity for strictly limiting her interests in life. I could see her going home and cozying up to the TV and letting it go at that.

A woman with a cart full of groceries came to her counter. I stepped aside and let the clerk do her checkering—occupying myself with a perusal of the available merchandise. Would Techsci shop here? It was only an overblown mom and pop store, and to feed the troops at the compound would probably require at least a supermarket.

When the woman pushed her cart full of bagged groceries out the door I took my place at the counter again.

"By the way, I'm Gil Yates—and I see by your tag you're Debbie—may I call you Debbie?"

She shrugged.

"Look," I said reaching for my wallet, "this is important to me—" I took out a hundred dollar bill and smoothed it on the counter with my hands. "Debbie, I'd like you to take this bill and do some thinking. If you remember anything helpful there are more where that came from. How many depends on how much you remember."

She looked at the hundred, then at me—I could tell her tongue was circling the inner surface of her teeth.

"I have a break coming up in about twenty minutes," she said. "I'll be out back."

I nodded. As I got to the front door I turned to

look at Debbie. She was on the telephone.

I felt later I should have known better. Chalk it up to inexperience. For as I was waiting at the back door of the market this moose came toward me. He was twice the size of Debbie and showed a lot of skin covering respectable musculature—all graced with stunning tattoos.

"You the guy's harassing my wife?" he asked.

"Excuse me?"

"You heard me." It was curious how he could be so menacing with so little effort.

"I may have heard you, but I haven't been harassing anyone. Your wife is the checker?" I asked, throwing my thumbs over my shoulder in the direction of the store. I was keeping my back to the wall as advised by reporter Larry Crouse.

"Yeah, and she thinks you're harassing her."

I wondered if she told him about the hundred dollars—I decided not to bring it up. "Well, I only asked her a couple of questions—showed her a picture."

"She don't want to answer no questions—so run along."

This guy was definitely not Harvard material, but then neither was I. I was amusing myself with this common thread when his sweetie appeared, lighting a cigarette en route. She gave me a quick you-still-here? look. And the moose answered her look. "I told him to run along."

She took a deep puff on the ciggy. I'd heard smoking took weight off people—Debbie was living proof you couldn't believe everything you heard.

I reached for my wallet and the moose jumped.

"Hey!" he grunted—

"Just my wallet," I said, holding it up for him to see. Debbie must have told him about the money—if she didn't, I thought it politic to introduce him to the idea. I took out five of the freshly minted hundreds I'd picked up for the purpose—and fanned them out in my hand like playing cards. Debbie took a deep dragnet on the cancer stick. The moose stepped closer—"Leon!" she snapped.

"Just wanted to see they's real," Leon said.

"They're real—" I said. "Want 'em?"

"What I have to do?" Leon asked.

"Depends," I said.

"On what?" he asked, cocking his head.

"What you *can* do." I picked up one of the bills—"Draw me a map to get to the Techsci place.

"Two—I.D. this picture—your wife thinks she looks familiar."

"I didn't say that!" The smoke was wafting out of her nostrils.

I held out two of the bills. "Okay," I said, "here's another just in case—"

"Let me see the pictures," Leon said.

I showed him—he looked at Debbie—she looked back. "What we have to do—jest say we recognize her and we get two hundred?"

"Another hundred. Debbie got the first one."

"What we got to do to get all of 'em?" he asked nodding at my hand of fanned bills.

"Get me in the compound—"

He whistled—"Don't want much, do you?"

Debbie's cigarette was gone—while she was

lighting the second she said, "You go in there all the time—"

"Yeah—if I took him I'd never go again—"

"You've been in the compound?"

He nodded. "Do some carpentry up there—time to time. Take 'em groceries when they get short."

Now I was feeling my heart bounce around. "You've seen this girl there?" I asked, flaunting the picture of Dawn—

"I seen her," he acknowledged. I passed over a hundred. He studied it as though he were a counterfeiting expert.

"I gotta go back in," Debbie said, stepping on another cigarette butt.

"Why don't you guys think it over?"

"You talking four hundred bucks?" he asked.

"Sure," I said. "Make it worth my while, I might go higher."

Leon licked his lips.

"Tell you what—why don't we meet for dinner. What's the best place around?"

"Oh, geez, I don't know," Debbie said. I think the reason she didn't know was she'd never been to any good restaurant. "I like Tess Barker's Grand Hotel," she said, "over in Los Olivos."

"Done!" I said. "What time do you get off?"

"Six."

"Shall we say six-thirty?"

"Seven-thirty—" Leon cut in. Maybe he thought I was emasculating him by consulting the little (big, actually) woman. "We gotta have time to talk it over—"

"Good enough."

"Oh, and hey," he said as he turned to go—"Dinner's on you, no matter what."

"Deal," I said, smiling to myself. I expect Leon was letting me know what a tough negotiator I was going to be up against.

11

The Grand Hotel in Los Olivos was grounded in the context of this tiny tourist stop. No crystal chandeliers and high ceilings. Just a quaint frame country house design with a pleasant parlor, dining room and a handful of rooms upstairs.

Since there didn't seem to be any run on the tables in the dining room, I opted to wait for the couple in the lobby.

And I waited—and waited. Seven-thirty came and went. And went, and went—I thought I could do a lot worse than spend the night here—and it was beginning to look like I'd have no choice. At eight-twenty, I booked a room. There was no pretense about having to search the reservations to make sure there was still a room left.

I decided to give them ten more minutes before retiring—leaving a note with the dining room manager that I could be reached in my room. When I turned, I saw the couple come in the front door—one at a time.

I couldn't call them a happy couple, because they looked like they had just had a knock down, drag strip fight, and there was no winner.

I went over to greet them as though I had no suspicions.

"Oh, hi!" I enthused. "Thanks for coming."

"We almost didn't," Debbie said, and I think it was followed by a sniffle, but I didn't look.

"Hope you're hungry."

The response was diverse grunts—his low and guttural, hers a chesty exasperation. But, unbowed, I led the way. They were here, weren't they? Obviously they wanted to eat—though from the looks of them I had to face the probability all that would come out of this for me was the opportunity to give them a free meal.

I am, I suspect, the last person to tell anyone how to dress, but in regard to Debbie, I would not, had I been asked, been above suggesting something a bit more demure. I won't say the form-fitting spandex concoction made her look like an overdressed buffalo, but the way it scooped under and gently hoisted her belly did smack of a pregnancy in the vicinity of eight and a half months, without that happy state being in the deck of cards.

Leon himself was showing a bit more tattoo than I would have orchestrated for the occasion, had I been in that position.

When the hostess sat us at our table, I couldn't help noticing the failed surreptitious once-over she gave my guests.

"So," I said, when the menus had been flopped in our hands, "how was your day?"

"Terrible!" Debbie exclaimed.

Leon shifted in search of a more comfortable hiding place. "We been disagreeing—mightily."

"Oh, how so?" I asked.

Leon nodded to his bride. "Wants me to jeopardize my job. Says you'll pay good, but then what when you're gone I don't have no more work? It ain't plentiful in these parts, so I say I can't help you—" he nodded at Debbie with a so-there flip of his overgrown head.

Debbie was sullen—"All I said was, he would make it worth your while." ·

"Yeah, and what's it worth to put me outta work for good?"

"You exaggerate. It's one job and it's almost over."

"Yeah, that's the other thing—I'm not going to have that much excuse to go back there much longer."

"Well," I said, "let's see what we can think up. Why don't you tell me how you get in—what you do when you're in there. What do you notice peculiar about the place?"

"I'm awful hungry," Leon said, and I didn't see any argument brewing in Debbie's direction.

"Good," I said, "let's order." We scanned our menus—they both opted for the steak smothered in blue cheese and fries. I had a slab of fish. A waiter took our orders with dispatch, then brought in a basket of bread and a plate of butter, which Debbie and Leon dispatched with aplomb. There were two refills before the meal came, during which Leon held forth on the details of his day at the camp.

"It's up the mountain road past the wineries a long way," he said. "I make the trip in my pickup. There's a gate and a lot of high chainlink fencing with razor wire on top. The guards at the gate always inspect my truck for I don't know what all—guns, bombs...stowaways," he said this last with a sidelong glance at Debbie. "Then I go in and work my trade on the mansion—out there where there's nothing. It's so out of place," he said, shaking his head.

"How far along is the house?" I asked.

"Putting the finishing touches on it now—so I don't even go everyday. We're working around the other trades."

"Who decides when you go?"

"My boss—the contractor."

"You going tomorrow?"

He shook his head. "Maybe day after—but they's no way I can get you in there."

"What's it like inside the compound?"

"Don't know much 'sides the house where I'm working. It's not like we get to roam around or anything."

"Where does Morgan live now?"

"A big mobile home. A ways from the mansion."

"See him a lot?"

"Some," he said, uneasily. "Comes in the mansion and barks his orders. Change this, change that."

"And you do the changes?"

"You bet. Sometimes four times...back and forth."

"He's erratic?"

"What's that?"

"Changes his mind a lot?"

"That he does."

"What's he look like?"

"Old—draggy—hey," Leon stopped himself. "You're paying for this info, right?"

I got out my wallet, withdrew two hundreds and passed them over. Debbie was watching closely with a "see-what-I-told-you" look on her face. Leon palmed the bills like a magician, and they disappeared somewhere under the table.

I brought out the pictures of Dawn and Suzanne. "Where did you see these two?"

"That there one—the young one, I seen her with Morgan when he comes around on his bitching trips."

"What do you think her job is? Secretary? Lover? Associate?"

"Dunno—gofer maybe—he'll bark something, and she'll scurry away like a scared cat."

"She doesn't look happy?"

He thought a moment. "Couldn't say," he said, "but I couldn't say she looked *un*happy either."

"See this one?" I asked, showing him the picture of Suzanne.

"Can't say I have." He frowned. "We don't wander from the job much. Lot of suspicion of outsiders—that place."

"You started to tell me what J. Kent Morgan looked like. Draggy, you said—what did you mean?"

"Yeah, he kind of drags around—hangdog like. His hair is long and stringy—kinda dirty. He's like an old man who's decided to hell with it—and let himself go, you know?"

I nodded. "What else?"

"Oh, rumor is he's in hiding. Afraid to be seen. They put his missus to jail, and they couldn't get their hands on him. Word is they'd love to nail him and he knows it. Grew a beard, wears huge shades."

"Does this girl always come with Morgan when he inspects your work?"

"Nah—sometimes other cadets. He calls his girls

cadets—sometimes he's alone," Leon said. "No patterns at that place. Everything is random."

"Except at the gate."

"Yeah—there it's pretty tight."

The food came. The military term chow down came to mind as Leon and Debbie dug in. My mother used to say she was so pleased to see people enjoy their food. She would have been ecstatic watching Debbie and Leon.

When Leon came up for air (I don't think Debbie ever did) I said, "So what would it take to get me in there?"

"Lotta money," he said, and I could swear he looked at me to see if I flinched.

I didn't.

"But," he added, "I can't think how's, the thing."

"How about as your helper—another carpenter—or a painter you are giving a ride to?"

"They'd check with Bud," he said, thoughtfully chewing.

"Bud?"

"My boss, the contractor. Paranoid's the word out there. Nobody's gettin' in or out without a damn good reason."

"A false floor in the truck bed?"

"What if we're caught? And how do you get from there to this chick?"

"Think you could bring this "chick" as you put it, out?"

"No way. Suicide."

"We'd be talking big money—"

"But that's like kidnapping. I ain't going to jail for no amount of money."

"Does she ever come out on her own?" I asked, looking at Debbie.

"Comes in the store sometimes."

"How often?"

"Not often. Seen her maybe twict in a year."

I frowned. That was too long a shot for my taste.

"Think of any enticement we could make to get her to come out?"

They both chewed thoughtfully, as though every chomp was a cylinder firing up their minds. Leon spoke. "I couldn't even get to her without arousing suspicion."

"That's the problem," Debbie said, as though she were conceding a long debated point.

"Okay," I said, after I had contributed some mastication of my own to the ritual. "How much?"

"How much what?" Leon asked, as though he were tuned to a different program.

"Money. How much money would it take either to get me in or get her out?"

Leon looked at Debbie. Debbie looked at Leon. The moment of truth was upon them and they were sore afraid.

"Yeah, well," Leon said, "it always comes down to money, doesn't it?"

I nodded because I couldn't think of an argument.

"Well," he licked his lips, glancing once again at the distaff, "I wouldn't kidnap her for no money, and I don't see any way of talking her out of there."

"Maybe she *wants* to get out."

"Yeah, well, you can deal with that—I can't."

"You'll get me in so I can talk to her?"

"Wait a minute," he said, "I can't guarantee anything. *If* I can get you in—for the right price—you'll be entirely on your own. You get caught and they tie you to me, I'm a gonner. These guys play for keeps, and I'm looking to live some more years."

"How about your tool chest? You have one on the truck?"

"Yeah."

"Put me in there? They ever check it?"

"In the beginning. Lately, I guess, they trust me."

"You could say I got in and you never saw me before in your life. I could get out without you knowing it. You wouldn't have any responsibility at all. Things went well, I'd climb back in before the end of the day. How does that sound?"

He looked at me levelly. I couldn't understand if it were a look of respect for my marvelous cunning, or a look at a man whose marbles were bouncing out of his ears, one by one.

Dessert was offered, it was not rejected. After they settled on the goopiest chocolate concoction offered and the waiter beat an obsequious retreat, Leon said—a trifle too loud for my taste: "Ten thousand dollars."

My eyebrows shot up—not because I was outraged by his demand, but because I didn't want him to know how modest I thought it was.

12

After agreeing to the ten grand, Leon consented to have lunch with me on the morrow to hammer out the details.

In my "high country" furnished room, I checked my voicemail. I had a message from Lajos Bohem. He sounded put out that I hadn't kept him abreast of the developments. That's what he said, "abreast." He was going to be high maintenance, I could see the handwriting on the ceiling without even looking up.

I didn't call him back. When I did call, I would time it so I got his voicemail instead of him. It would be more pleasant. Lajos Bohem was a guy who could make my father-in-law look like a prince among us folks.

Leon and I met at a simple restaurant in Santa Ynez. Leon thought it would be prudent not to be seen with me anywhere more than once.

After I agreed to the ten thousand payment I thought it politic and prudent to make some stipulations. First I would give him half up front when I climbed in his toolbox, and half when I arrived back in Los Olivos in one piece.

Leon argued that when he had gotten me inside the compound he would have fulfilled his obligation. He could make no guarantees about getting me back, and in fact could almost guarantee I *wouldn't* be coming back.

"Easier to break into the White House in Washington," was the way he put it. "They have these guards all over the place. No way can you *move* in there and not get caught."

"On the other hand," I said, "I give you ten grand up front, what guarantee do I have I'll get anywhere near the Techsci compound? You could dump me in Timbuktu and I couldn't get back in time to stop payment on the check."

"Cashier's check," he said, with a stolid intake of breath.

Since he knew better than I, and I couldn't argue his point about not getting out, we compromised. I would give him a five thousand dollar cashier's check when I crawled into his pickup truck tool box. I would have another five thousand dollar check, which I would show to him before I crawled in the box. When I opened the lid—after Leon was some safe distance away and saw I was in the compound as he was to describe and diagram for me, I would leave the check in the box. If there was no check there, he would personally blow the whistle on me. He made it abundantly clear he wouldn't give a nickel for my life in the hands of Techsci elite storm troops.

Leon made me agree to not acknowledge any relationship between us. If caught I would say I had stowed away in his toolbox without his knowledge.

He drew me a map of the Techsci compound. The working area of the two-hundred plus acres was in the form of a "T." This land area was surrounded by the ten-foot fence. The long trunk of the "T" was about two miles long and began at the road with a guardhouse. The guards were armed with automatic rifles. Lately they waved him through, but they could resume the checks anytime. If we passed the first guardhouse, we would drive about a mile up a private road to another guardhouse where we could also be subject to inspection. If we passed scrutiny, we would be waved through, into the guts of the compound. The dormitory was on the left, on the right of the road was an all-purpose building. At that point we will have arrived at the top cross bar of the "T." The construction project—a twenty-five room mansion to be occupied by the big man and indeterminate others was on the left. This mansion had been under construction for over three years and every time the construction workers thought they were near completion, J. Kent Morgan would breeze through the house, wave his arms and bark orders to tear this wing down, to add a room here, consolidate rooms there, change the molding on the doors and windows—anything you could change, Morgan wanted changed.

"Lifetime full employment for carpenters," Leon said with a rueful smile.

If one turned right at the top center of the "T" and drove a half mile or so, one would come to the heavily guarded "temporary" living quarters of J. Kent Morgan, head honcho of Techsci. It was a gussied up forty-foot mobile home.

For further self-preservation, Leon had me copy his map in my own hand, then destroyed his rendering.

Leon wanted to lock the toolbox after I was inside it. For various and obvious reasons I didn't like the sound of that. He thought it would be an extra precaution—if the goons at the gate asked to see inside the box he could fish around for the key—curse and say he left it at home and turn around to go home to get it. Though this trip would be over thirty miles, Leon apparently didn't think anyone would be suspicious.

"Let them be suspicious," was his answer to that. "It's better than being locked up and tortured by those goons."

I'll say this for Leon, he seemed to show a flair for this kind of clandestine activity.

"But," I said, "how are we going to claim I was a stowaway if the box is locked from the outside?"

That seemed to perplex Leon for a moment. "Different people," he said at last.

"Different people? What's that mean?"

"You'll be locked till we get inside the gates. That's two miles after I unlock the box. If you're caught, you'll be a stowaway."

"You don't think they'll compare notes?"

"Not before I can get out of there. They're two miles apart."

"With or without me?"

He looked at me with a sinister smile. "That's on the money," he said.

For my foray into the Techsci compound, I drove to Santa Barbara and I stocked up on several essentials: a digital camera—a Sony DSC-U10 cyber shot—smaller than four inches by two inches by one inch, so it fit right in my pocket. The best news was the film was the size of a truncated stick of gum, could hold hundreds of pictures and weighed next to nothing.

When I entered the film shop the salesman asked me if I needed help, then paused and said, "or are you beyond it?" which I thought was screamingly funny— and could only have been funnier had it been at someone else's expense. In the process of conning me into my purchases, he told me I was getting a one point three megapixel image sensor. That may be a concept some people can grasp, but I was not among them. I got some extra one hundred twenty-eight megabyte film, some cheapo sixteen megabyte film, and a reader to view the digital pictures from, then fled the premises for under four hundred bucks and appropriate gratitude for getting out with my skin. I decided to mail the reader to Bohem's secretary—after all, it was the mogul who had to see the pictures so I could get my pay.

To assuage my dietary dilemma, I bought a couple of high-energy bars and a canteen that would fit flat against my hip. I felt outfitted worthy of a D-Day invasion, but I was going as a photographer, not as a rifleman.

I'd once asked Daddybucks if he didn't think a cell phone would make me more efficient as a property manager to God's banker. He did not. Obviously he didn't want to spend the money. But on further reflection it was for the best. I wanted it for my secret line of work—private investigation. One of the strong points of my underground line was top secrecy. I'd heard cell phones could be listened in on, and then there's the unappetizing fact that Daddybucks would get the bill and go over it with a fancy-toothed comb. You wouldn't think that a guy that rich would be so cheap with his pennies, but you'd think wrong.

My next stop was a shoemaker who scoffed at my idea until I told him the simple act on his part would be worth one hundred dollars to me. That caught his interest, but it didn't make him less grumpy.

I don't know why this part of my preparation started me thinking of the inherent danger of what I was doing. Not being a macho stud in real life—some wags might even say I was henpecked—I came into this avocation quite by accident—the same wags, if they'd known about my anonymous conversion from milque-toast to dashing private eye (revealed in *The Missing Link*), would assay that I was a few marbles short of a tournament.

That night before our early morning assault on the Techsci beachhead, after I was sure Lajos Bohem had gone home, I placed a call to his office.

Wouldn't you know, he grabbed it on the first ring before I'd had time to completely rehearse the message I was going to deposit on his voicemail.

"Lajos?" I said, not able to believe my ill-luck, hoping there was some mistake.

"Yaytz—it's about time. I don't pay tat kind of money to be eegnored. What is going on? Haf you found tem?"

"I'm getting close," I said, "a lot closer than I expected to so soon."

"Tat's good news," he gloated. I could just see him with his hand on his hip, clenching his cigarette holder between his teeth and grinning from floppy ear to floppy ear. I wished at that moment that I had more enthusiasm for the case. How could *anyone* work for this creep? I almost hoped I would fail. Money may not be precisely the root of all evil, but it is available in the service of many evil things—to wit: my mission to return to Schlockmeister Lajos Bohem his two women who, showing more sense than he has, have broken free from him and his sinister sphere.

"Where are you?" Lajos demanded in that oleaginous way he had of ingratiating that only grated on me.

"Close," I said. "I expect to have pictures for you soon."

"Peectures? I want my wife and leetle girl."

Your little girl is not so little anymore, I thought, but knew better than to impart this startling intelligence to this baboon. "You will remember the first phase is I locate them and offer you proof. You take it from there."

"But you said you would bring tem home."

"If I could—and it would be a lot more expensive. If people don't want to go somewhere, you can't make them."

"But you can do tah meeracle. You haf tah reputation."

But, do I want to? I asked myself, and in spite of the great pot of gold at the end of the rainstorm, I wasn't sure. I decided to lay it on thick—"Lajos," I said, "this mission *is* the most dangerous I have ever undertaken. I have probably underpriced it—I will pursue the subjects to the best of my ability commensurate with my ultimate safety. Your patience and cooperation will be appreciated. You will be first to hear of any news I have."

"So tell me what you are doing. Keep me abreast."

"Sorry," I said. "I don't share the process, only the result."

"Meester Yaytz—I haf lot of money riding on you."

"You have *nothing* riding on me. My expenses are already high and I get not a penny from you without results, so please let's not get too high and mighty. I don't respond well to being shoved. I'll let you know."

"When?" he asked.

But I cut him off.

As I contemplated the efficacy of sleep as opposed to plotting and planning my strategy for the morrow, I began to have more fears. My mission was simple enough. Photograph the subject *in situ*. Depending how complex that proved to be, I could opt for the second phase (and much more money). I realized I would be faced with a couple of women who would be strongly opposed to any suggestion that they return to their hearth and home and the smothering arms of the legendary Lajos Bohem.

But even as I decided sleep would be in my best interests, as I should be obliged to be as alert as possible in the morning, that blessed state was not easily achieved. As usual, the more fiercely one pursued the unconscious state, the more elusive it became.

It was cold in the morning when Leon picked me up in his old pickup. I climbed in the cab and subjected myself to the wit and wisdom of Leon—after I handed over the first check and showed him the second.

The sun was just peaking over the mountains as we pulled off the main road onto a dirt road.

"This is it," Leon said. "Your big moment. Good luck to both of us."

It didn't really hit me until I was in the toolbox that this had to be one of the most foolhardy jobs I had ever undertaken. When Leon was spreading his doom and gloom I thought he was just trying to prepare me for the remote worst. Now, with the reality of the womb-like rationale, I was beginning to wonder if Leon might be telling the truth. The Journalist, Larry Crouse, had certainly painted a bleak picture of Techsci's roughhousing, but I just couldn't imagine any of this affecting me—a rank outsider. I wasn't, after all, a whistle blowing ex-member. But I was armed with a small camera I hoped would be invisible to the troops—a hope Leon scoffed at as "dreaming."

It must, in fairness, be admitted, the shocks on Leon's pickup had seen better days and my liver got a good shaking on the country roads we bounced over.

The negotiated scenario was this: Leon would lock me in on a deserted side street after we left the main road. I would have a hammer and saw with me for insurance—when we got near the mansion under construction in the Techsci compound, Leon would park with maximum privacy (not, apparently, a piece of pie to achieve) and when the coast was clear, unlock the box. If that were unsafe, he would simply let me cooped up in there until he felt I would be unobserved.

When I left the box I would leave the five thousand dollar balance behind and re-lock the box.

I could feel and sense our approach to the first gate—the ninety degree turn, the slow down, the muttered pleasantries. I had the sense we were crossing the border of an unfriendly country. My mind was reeling with all the things that could go wrong. I pictured myself hanging from wall mounted chains with bloodhounds yipping and nipping at my feet. The cold darkness of my tomb was closing in on me, and I feared my Edgar Allen Poe heartbeat would be a dead giveaway to the guards at the gate.

We drove a good distance, then made a left turn of ninety degrees and after a further distance we rolled to a stop. The two short and one long tap on my coffin were not forthcoming, so I realized there must be some inhibitor—some guard with his automatic machine gun at the ready roaming the premises. I was settling into resignation of my untenable position and deciding maybe I'd be better off staying in this tomb and returning with Leon at the end of the day, five thousand dollars poorer. Leon would fight for the other five but I would make a strong case for the return of the other five because I had not technically been delivered to my destination since I couldn't leave the toolbox.

I was a little disappointed in myself because I wasn't more disappointed. Perhaps with this creepy danger staring me in the face—and risk that I did not relish—just perhaps it was time to throw it all over and tend to my palms and cycads. I was never cut out to be a rich man.

Then I heard the rap on the toolbox. I heard the key in the lock, the simple metal on metal, the rudimentary turning of the tumblers, the clicking of the releases of the locking metal and the sudden invasion of light into my box, the adjustment of my eyes to a rather blinding sun. By the time I made the adjustment, Leon was nowhere to be seen. All I saw was a vast barren landscape, the mansion under construction in the distance and a road that seemed to lead to nowhere.

13

I had memorized the map of Techsci, but I had
it in my pocket just in case I had a memory lapse.
Before I started walking in the direction of the all purpose building, I scanned the landscape. I didn't see any
cover. My only hope was to look like I belonged. What
I had going for me was I was the kind of generic guy,
unassuming and unthreatening, who could blend into
the woodwork—if only there had been some woodwork
to blend into.

I decided to haul myself down the road.
Anything else would have been more suspicious. I
moved unmolested and, as far as I knew, undetected,
down the road to the center of activity, where I hoped I
would have the opportunity to spy Dawn and Suzanne
and snap some pictures surreptitiously.

It seemed a long way to the center complex. I
wondered if this dead brown wasteland was some kind
of metaphor for Techsci and what I had come to—
remote, barren and uninviting.

Of course I had to wonder what I would do
when I got there—say "Hi, I'm Gil Yates and I just

wandered across the plain and over your ten-foot chain-link fence iced with the razor wire, and I wondered if you could spare me a glass of water." At which time I would sit down with the constabulary and shoot the gentle wind and before I knew it would slip Dawn and Suzanne Bohem into the conversation—have them run out to meet me, pose for pictures and have them enthuse as how they would like nothing more than a tearful reunion with old Lajos Bohem himself. Sure, I'd be glad to arrange that, and we would all exit the double gates of this paradise of paranoia waving happily at the guards who returned the pleasantries.

Neat.

But not, of course, to be.

As soon as I got into sight of the monolith that must have been the dormitory and the meeting center across the road, I removed the tiny camera stealthily from my pocket and shot a couple of pictures of the buildings, which looked like basic ski-country housing with a distinct homemade quality about them. All seemed quiet in the environs of these paste-up jobs—perhaps it was breakfast time and the troops were all in one place. I could go to the window and photo the group, pick up my camera, climb back in the toolbox, head home and collect my phase one fee.

Neat.

But, as I said, not to be.

Luck was still with me. I approached the building with a bizarre mixture of stealth and bravado, torn between wanting to look like I belonged and hiding. As I got close to the monolith, I wondered why the leaders of this band had not seen fit to plant some trees to break the monotony. Then I wondered if I wasn't the reason. One of the mythical millions like me who would hide in the bushes to invade the privacy of the penitents.

I angled myself so I could look in the window without being in the line of vision of most of the crowd. I scanned the room, The revelers looked glum—like the denizens of Nevada gambling parlors. I didn't peg them for intellectuals, but they weren't derelicts either. But what was their function here? Aiding and abetting the hiding of J. Kent Morgan? Or is there some hidden pretense to get the competing factions close to the Kingmaker?

I couldn't get over the feeling these faces were forlorn. My focus shifted from one to the other in search of Dawn and Suzanne. There didn't seem too many the age of Dawn. Nor could I find anyone at the tables resembling Suzanne. It was almost a fluke that I saw her. For some reason I had not expected to see her behind the serving table, slinging the hash, so to speak. I wish I could report she looked happy. Instead she looked haggard and ten years older than the picture presented to me by her estranged husband.

Quickly I fired three shots of Suzanne with her oatmeal scoop at the ready. I was thinking that was the best I could do and save my skin. I was about to pocket my camera when I saw this young woman enter the room carrying an empty tray. Before I could get my camera back she disappeared through a door—probably to the kitchen.

Just as it occurred to me to shift to another window where I might observe my Dawn hopeful, she came back into the dining room carrying a load of bowls to the counter where she deposited them in front of her mother. My camera did its bit, and I got untold shots of the mother and daughter penitents.

Then I photographed the group to get the largest participation with the least chance of anyone seeing me.

The digital camera gave me the opportunity to shoot a lot of pictures, and when I thought I had covered the waterfront I shut down the photography wing of the operation, popped the chewing gum stick chip out of the camera, checked the terrain to see if I were being observed, then satisfied that I was still blissfully alone, wrapped the "film" in plastic wrap and inserted it between the sole and the floor of the shoe that the shoemaker in Santa Barbara had altered for me. I then added a touch of epoxy to seal the shoe.

Next step was to put the smaller capacity sixteen megabite film in the camera and take some innocuous shots of the two buildings that I could see—the all-purpose dining hall, meeting room where I stood and the dormitory across the road. I added a few of the fencing. I finished in the nickel of time and put the camera in my pocket just as the first diners were exiting the dining room for the dormitory. Some staying back to do, I suppose, their daily chores in the heartbeat of the operation.

I had to make a snap decision. Did I try and blend in with the sparse groups that were sauntering down the road, or did I try to move to the relatively blind side of the building without being noticed through the windows? I chose the latter as the less risky because it had the added benefit of scoping out other parts of the building. I compromised—went around the building—saw windows with shades drawn—and positioned myself so I could audit the exodus from the dining room, most of whom seemed destined for the dorms.

It seemed like everyone and then some must have left the building and no sign of Dawn or Suzanne. I circled the building without gaining much information on the innards. The dining room was virtually empty with a few unidentified stragglers hunched over cups of coffee and looking generally morose.

Then it happened—my big break. Dawn and Suzanne came out the door of the building at a brisk clip. I moved as fast as I could without drawing suspicion and fell in step beside them—Suzanne next to me, Dawn on her other side.

"Hi," I said, stretching my ingenuity to its outer limits.

They looked over at me in unison. Instead of responding with a hi of their own (perhaps they weren't all that creative) Suzanne said, "Who are you?"

"I'm Gil Yates," I said amiably.

"You new here?" Suzanne was doing the talking.

"You might say that."

"What's your function?"

"Just trying to get along," I said.

She nodded. Dawn looked straight ahead.

"Like it here?" I asked.

I noticed a stiffening of the musculature of both women.

"We love it," Dawn said, protesting too much.

"So if you really don't, why do you stay?"

"I *said* we *love* it," Dawn insisted.

"Well, I know why I'm here, but I just wondered about two beautiful women like yourselves. I mean, all you have to do is look around too see you are far and away the most beautiful on campus." It worked—they loosened up, smiled and seemed to slow their step as if to give more time for additional flattery. Say something nice in the realm of believability, and you have created an instant friend. Only the most jaded could claim any immunity to compliments.

"Any chance you want to leave here?"

"No—why?"

"Lot of people do, I hear."

"Not us," Dawn said.

"So...this is a good life for you, is it? Kitchen work?"

"It's okay—" Suzanne said.

"Better than the alternative," Dawn said.

"Oh, what's that?"

"You don't want to know."

"Little rough at home, was it?" I asked in my most friendly manner.

"You could say that," she said.

Dawn was more aloof. "Who are you, anyway?"

"Gil Yates," I said again, cheerfully.

"How long have you been here?"

"My first day, actually."

"We aren't taking anybody new," Dawn said, suspicion coating her lips.

"I'm in luck then," I said—"or am I? I'm not getting a real positive feeling so far."

We came to the dormitory door and I had to make a decision to follow them in or beat a tactful retreat. I should have taken my film, strolled back to the toolbox and crawled in, but the extra money and the thrill of the chase clouded my judgment. I knew I was about to lose them, knew I wouldn't have another chance, so I blurted, "Lajos would like to see you. Make it worth your while financially—a short visit is all that's called for. I'll take you and guarantee your safe return—if you want to come back here—"

I don't know what I expected, but what I got was not it. They looked at me as though I were a child-molesting axe-murderer, and literally *ran* into the dormitory, slamming the door in my face.

Well, I had my pictures, I earned my first phase fee, perhaps that would be enough this time around. I realized I could have been more subtle, but I didn't see the opportunity anywhere on the horizon. My thoughts turned to getting back to my escape vehicle for my safe egress from this prison.

I started back in the direction of the mansion under construction, sauntering along the road as though I belonged. I kept an eye peeled on the fence, expecting to see guards patrolling.

I didn't see any guards at the fence, but before I reached the pickup where I could climb into my safe haven, I heard the sounds of a speeding car behind me. I knew better than to look, but kept on at my leisurely pace—plain old Gil Yates without a care in the world.

The car screeched to a halt, doors flung open and three sinister looking guards, each with skin saving Uzi's pointed at plain old me, hopped out and surrounded me with an embarrassing ease.

I had to suppress a laugh—they looked like guys who might come out of Morgan's one hundred seventy-six billion year-old civilization—an epoch that vanished, no doubt, because they didn't have the benefit of the wit and wisdom of chairman Morgan to get released of the garbage of the inner soul.

"What are you doing here?"

"Just a newspaper reporter looking for a story—"

"How did you get in?"

I pasted a weak smile on my face—"You know a reporter can't reveal his sources."

The ring leader waved his Uzi at the car. "Get in," he said.

I was just about to oblige when I felt the butt of another automatic rifle slam against my back, propelling me in the desired direction. I slammed against the car and was pushed into the rear seat with what I considered unnecessary, yea even brutal force. When all the bozos were in, we drove off.

14

The goons whisked me away to the all purpose clump of a building. The way they manhandled me led me to believe they had experience but no finesse.

The detention center was the way they referred to the quaint windowless room into which I was unceremoniously thrown, but not before I was outfitted in regular Techsci chains (patent pending). To say that the iron getup was overkill would be overkill. The chains crisscrossed my body from leg irons to shoulders on down to handcuffs. I felt like a metallic hourglass with the sand running out.

Of course they confiscated my camera and the diversion film and left me my shoes so I'd have something to be self-conscious about.

"Boss frowns on these things," the big guy said. "Techsci is our universe.

The big surprise was I was being "detained" with another party, a young woman, as near as I could tell, because she had been given the same chain treatment I had. On closer scrutiny she had a slight frame and a broad, sturdy face—not what you would call a classic beauty.

One of my early thoughts was this dungeon-like room must have been designed with a forethought, the powers having foreseen the need for a prison in this "religion." I wondered if there were such a thing as a board of prison examiners and what they would say if they saw this place. It was just a windowless room with a regular door. They were counting on the chains to do the trick. A naked light bulb of dim wattage hung over the center of the room.

On leaving me with this hapless Madonna, the guard said, "It is forbidden to talk in here."

As soon as the door clicked shut and we could hear the locks click into place, my companion said, *sotto voce*, "These people are crazy."

"Why are you here?" I whispered.

"Disobedience," she snickered, "the big man accused me of putting starch in his shirts. Had a real meltdown over it."

"Did you?"

"No. All in his mind—like everything else. By the way, I'm Irene."

"Hi. Gil."

"How'd you rate this royal treatment?"

"Wanted to do a newspaper story."

"They don't like scrutiny—for good reasons."

"Any civil rights lawyers, trials, anything?"

She laughed. "That's a good one. J. Kent is the law here. He's also paranoid, so don't look at him cross-eyed."

There was a terrifying rap on the door. The

strong but muffled voice cut through the solid core—
"No talking!" Irene rolled her eyes. "They're crazy,"
she said again.

After a descent interval of silence, I whispered,
"How long have you been here?"

"Couple days. I lose track."

"Time flies when you're having fun."

"Yeah."

"What's it like here—outside this cell?"

"Russia," she said. "Totalitarianism, terror," she
rattled her chains and rattled a lugubrious laugh.

"So why are so many here?"

"Brainwashing," she said. "Expensive brainwashing."

The clanging of opening locks cut off the conversation. The door flung open in anger by Mr. Macho.
"I *said* no talking. I mean *no* talking!"

"Say," I said, "I'd like to call a lawyer."

"Yeah, dream on."

"I have rights," I said.

"This is not that kind of place," he said. Mr.
Macho came over to me, his Uzi at the ready—I wondered if he were such a poor shot that multiple bullets
would be necessary to stop me—he pulled me roughly
to my feet and said—"Come on."

He hauled me hobbling and clanking into
another room that had windows, but they were covered
with shades and heavy curtains. There was a table in the
center of the room with chairs around it. After I was
deposited in a chair, secure in my chains, he stood
behind me like some novice upstart from a third world
dictatorship.

It wasn't long before a creepy guy came in the room. He had sunken eyes and curvature of the spine and a dark buzz cut which helped put me in mind of a guy who had been dishonorably discharged from the marines on a morals charge.

He sat down and stared at me as though that would break me and send me groveling to the floor at his feet, spewing uncontrollably my *mea culpa*.

When he finally spoke it was through clenched, capped teeth with an eerie attempt at intimidation, "What are you doing here?" he demanded.

"Three goons jumped out of a car at me, drove me here—chained me." I wiggled my hands so he wouldn't miss the point.

"*Why* are you here?"

"I just told you."

"Don't get smart with me," he said with his sinister deadpan. "It won't help you. Why were you trespassing on our property?"

"Are you accusing me of a crime?"

"Trespassing's a crime."

"Then I shouldn't suppose you'd object to me calling a lawyer."

He slammed his hand on the table. "The Neeleys put you here, didn't they?"

"Who?"

"Don't be cute."

"Thank you."

The hand slammed again. "You think I'm stupid?"

"I hardly know you—"

He nodded as though he were the sage of

Techsci, and he was on to me, big time. "You know I can keep you here in chains till you rot."

"One of the tenets of your religion, is it?"

The creep didn't cotton to me, this was evident. But then, I didn't cotton to him, either. I decided at this juncture I should oyster up and not share any goodies with him. Let him reveal something before I did.

"How long have you known Neeley?" he said.

I shrugged.

"What is he paying you?"

"Ask him," I said. "Does he know I'm in here?" I asked.

When he tired of playing cat and rat with me he abruptly left without a word and the goon prodded me back to my cell, where Irene and I shared a meal that wouldn't send any dog into ecstasy.

I whispered a synopsis of my audience with the creep.

"Savage," she said. "He's jockeying for the takeover. Morgan has one foot in a mental institution, the other in the grave and, and someone's going to get his hands on a lot of bucks."

"Who is Neeley?" The name sounded familiar.

"The other contender. Morgan's companion. Savage probably thinks he hired you to investigate him. I told you. *Every*body is paranoid. Savage wouldn't be true to his nature if he didn't suspect you were a plant. *They* plant people everywhere and are suspicious of everyone. That's why this place supposedly has only the most loyal of lackeys.

"So what are you doing here?" she asked, and I was jarred by the timing. Could she have been a plant?

How perfect—and convenient—to have her in the same cell. The only thing that assuaged my suspicion was the timing. How they would have had the time to get her in these chains between the time of my snatch and my deposit in this Shangri-la. All the same, I'd better play the old cards close to my shirt.

"Secret mission," I said with a smug humor in my smile.

"Oh," she said, "yeah, I get it. You think I'm a plant, and I don't blame you—that's par for the course around here. It's okay—I don't need to know anything. I've been around long enough so I can write the scenarios. Let me write yours—don't tell me if I'm right or wrong. Someone's here you want to get out. They come in two types—those that want to get out, and those who don't. Yours are probably in the last category or you'd be out of here by now."

"You don't buy that I'm a newspaper man trying to get a story?"

"I don't buy it, no. Is any story worth this fate?"

"Should be safer than crawling on your belly in a foxhole to get a war story."

"Isn't," she said with a quaint finality.

"So how much money you figure these guys are after? If they get control?"

"Phew," she whistled quietly, "untold sums—nobody knows, but if you extrapolate the estimated suckers by the average tariff, you have *big* bucks."

"A hundred million?"

"Huh!" she scoffed. "Petty cash in this operation. Well, mark my words, you'll get a surreptitious visit from Vic Neeley."

"Any chance I'll see the big man?"

"Doubt it. He's scared of his shadow now. Never leaves the compound. Hardly moves from his trailer. Then only to kibitz in the construction of the mansion. You ever hear of Winchester mansion in San Jose?"

"Yeah. The widow Winchester raking in all that money on weapons of killing built room after room on the house—stairways going to nowhere—in an effort to appease the spirits."

"To keep the grim reaper out of her hair," she said. "Well, this operation reminds me of that. They build a perfectly sumptuous house for him and he can't keep from tinkering with it—then sometimes even tinkering back. I think he thinks he'll live as long as he keeps building. Just like old lady Winchester did."

"What do you think?"

She made a face in the ray of the naked light which gave her an ethereal cast. "I'm not superstitious," she said with a sanitized laugh. "Then how did I wind up in this place? You may well ask. Believe me, I ask the same question, over and over."

There was another pounding on the door. "*No talking!*"

We fell silent until we heard footsteps recede from the door.

"Do you know Dawn Bohem—and Suzanne Bohem?"

"Sure. You get to know most everybody after a time."

"What do you make of them? They glad to be here?"

"There's a difference between knowing someone and knowing them well. I don't know them well. Dawn and I were cadets together. She's a good kid, I guess. Not too high on her father, I gather—" she shrugged— "Not that unusual, I guess."

"You high on your father?"

"Never knew him. He hightailed it out of there when I was a pup. Never looked back. But my mother being what she is, I can hardly blame him."

"Got solace in the club, did you?"

"For a while. Till I came to my senses and started asking questions—simple questions, like what? and why? And I wasn't satisfied with the answers. But by then I was so deep in the sham, I couldn't get out. I wasn't good at hiding my skepticism, and that's death around here. The folly is not strong enough to withstand doubting Thomases. Catholicism has withstood millennia of doubters. You'd think Techsci would collapse ten minutes after the first doubt was expressed."

"So what do you think is in store for us?"

She shrugged. "I sit here until I recant. Unhappily, there is no one looking for me—my mother couldn't care less. Never had a real boyfriend. This was my salvation. Salivation was more like it. You—" she said—"are a different matter. I don't have any experience with your type. Newspaper reporter," she scoffed. "A likely story—but with the paranoia rampant around here, I might give a different story—something less threatening."

"Like what?"

"Oh, you're looking for a lost relative or something. Acting on a tip or a hunch. No thought of escape—just want a tearful reunion and the satisfaction of knowing they are alive."

"Excellent idea," I said.

Irene rang a bell—an old-fashioned thing with a clapper and in due time a guard came in to take her to the bathroom. Free of her company, my mind took several turns:

1. Irene didn't have to be a plant, the room was doubtlessly bugged.

2. I could kiss goodbye my ten grand—and how could I complain? Leon had worked the impossible and gotten me into the Techsci compound. Of course, the way things worked out, I would have been better off not having gotten in because I didn't see any way out with my senses and body intact.

3. I wondered how long it would be before Lajos Bohem and Tyranny Rex and Elbert August Wemple Realtor Ass. would miss me and start the search process. I speculated with Lajos Bohem it would be a matter of days—with Tyranny Rex weeks—Elbert August Wemple months, if at all.

The guard who brought Irene back, took me out.

As we crossed paths, she whispered, "It's Neeley."

15

Vic Neeley introduced himself by that name, shook my hand and managed a broad, ingratiating smile to boot. I thought instantly of the good cop (Neeley) bad cop (Savage) routine. You know the game where the bad guy is hard and unfriendly to the suspect, then the good guy comes in and pretends to be the suspect's friend.

"Well, I guess these are not the most comfortable accommodations you've had in your life," Vic Neeley began after he made a show of seeing me comfortably in a chair. He didn't seem to notice my chains. He was at all times affable and solicitous of my comfort—"I'm going to see what I can do to change this inconvenience. You don't look like a happy camper to me, and Techsci wants happy campers."

I looked at him as though expecting he was going to reveal himself at any moment as the real Jesus Christ, and I didn't want to miss a minute of it. "Those are nice sentiments," I said during a lull in your my-well-being-is-paramount litany, "just a little hard for me to take seriously while I'm detained in chains."

"Yes, yes," he said with a sympathetic nod, "I'm going to get you out—just as soon as I can. But you have to help me. There's a lot of resistance around here."

"Overcome it," I muttered.

"I'm trying," he said. "But you have breached our security rather seriously and we'd just like to—" he spread his hands out wide—"understand where you're coming from—and *why?*"

I nodded, but didn't say anything.

"Does your surprise presence here—on private property that no little effort has been made to let the public know *is very private*—have anything to do with Mr. Savage and his associates?"

"If my memory has not failed—and God knows under these circumstances," (I rattled my chains) "anything is possible—he—that is Mr. Savage—asked the same thing about you."

Neeley's look told me he thought that was a likely story. I, in the meantime searching for some way to use this rivalry to my benefit—without winding up with concrete shoes in the briny deep. "What did he say, exactly?"

"Well," I said, playing for time, "yes...sure— but, can you...I'm just wondering out loud now—can you possibly put yourself in my chains—so to speak? Looks to me—and you know I could be wrong—looks to me like you have some factions in this concentration camp." I watched his face. He wasn't covering his disappointment. "I am, it must be admitted, a man who is not a complete stranger to self-interest and that passing acquaintance with said self-interest encourages me to parcel my favors as would a young virgin at a fraternity party. So…not to be crude about it or anything…I was just idly wondering what…if anything…was in it for me?"

He tried to cover his absolute power with an I'm-your-pal smile. "I assume you wouldn't object to getting out of here."

"With or without the chains?"

"Too-shay," he said, giving me a stalwart thumbs up. "The way to get out of the dugout is to play ball."

Lord, he was a baseball fan. I was put out at that, baseball not being an area of my expertise, I couldn't swap batting averages with him, though in the circumstances, he was obviously the heavy hitter and I'd be lucky to get off the occasional bunt. "I'm afraid," I said, "I'm a raw rookie at baseball—"

He checked me out to verify my belief in my words. "I'm going to make a home-run hitter out of you. I'm on your side. I want to get you out of here."

I thrust my chained hands toward him. "You got the key?"

He held up a hand. "In good time," he said, smiling like a real pal.

"When is that?"

"In good time," he repeated. "Now, why don't you just tell me how Mr. Savage contacted you?"

"Oh—" I said, "now you're getting personal."

"Yes, I suppose you could say being chained in that room is personal—so it will take the personal to get you out."

"Why does any of this matter?"

"Matter? Techsci is a large and vibrant organization. Our chief is not what he used to be. An orderly transition is vital. The only question is who to transfer it to."

"That brutal Savage, or mister nice guy like you?"

"Oh, ho—you're not a slow learner after all."

"Lot of money at stake, I imagine."

Again, a laser look that threatened to burn through my soul. "It's not about money," he said, "it's about the fate of mankind."

Oh, my, I thought: Delusions. "What *is* the fate of mankind?"

"Without Techsci, it isn't good," he intoned like a hell-fire-and-brimstone minister on wind down.

"I'll take your word for it." (I thought I was being magnanimous). "But the question is—what do you want from me—and what will you give for it?"

He smiled again, and when he did his dimples lit up like the Lincoln memorial at night. "I suppose any answer to that question will depend on what you know and how badly you want to get out of here with your skin."

"My skin is one of my favorite parts."

"So save it—start talking." He was over the good cop part.

"Yeah, sure," I said. "But I talk to you, your cohort might not like it. He might want me to talk to him." I shrugged, trying to convey a touch of leverage.

"All right," he said. "What *can* you tell me?"

"I can tell you this kidnapping of me will not put smiles on the faces of any legally constituted representatives of the people."

"Yes, and that's not news to anybody. I have enough confidence in your good sense. My associate, Mr. Savage, has more of a skeptical nature. I would certainly hope that he wouldn't think it necessary to buy your silence with some extreme measure. But I can't speak for him."

"All right," I said. "Let me speak to the head man—"

"Mr. Morgan, himself?"

I nodded.

He chuckled. "Not bloody likely," he said. "He sees no one outside of Techsci."

"Can't hurt him in these chains. I should think it would be in your best interests to have me out of here."

"I agree—once we know what you're doing in here in the first place."

My silence was effective—his body language seemed to be collapsing in on itself.

"I'll tell the chief," I said.

Vic Neeley held me in his gaze for an eternity. I wasn't going anywhere in a hurry, so I gazed back.

He stood up. I saw no joy on his face. "I'll see what I can do," he said, and the guard took me back to my cellmate.

She was eager to hear what happened. I gestured to the unknown electronic listening devices, so we sat close and whispered. I couched my information, realizing she could still be a spy.

We schmoozed a while about the terrors wrought in the name of religious purity, which Irene characterized as asinine and all pervasive paranoia.

"Think there's any way I could talk to Dawn

and Suzanne? Get word to them to visit you here?" Perhaps a stupid move, but my trust knew no bounds.

She wrinkled her nose. "Not likely. There's a stigma visiting an outcast. Guilt by association kind of thing."

The guard brought our evening "meal." Day old bread that was so shot full of preservatives it would never get stale. And beans boiled to a fair-thee-well. We ate in silence, neither of us considering the implications of the fare.

Eating in chains was a challenge. To get the food in our mouths we had to bend our heads. One of the rationales for the beans was we didn't have to cut anything. Except, of course, later, in a manner of speaking, the cheese.

"What kind of people are the Bohems?" I asked at last.

She rubbed her nose on her arm by bending her head. "I spent more time around Dawn. She's strange, I guess. Guarded. Some mysterious trauma in her past, I gather."

"Know what?"

"Not really. I never was interested enough to press her. Don't have any idea she'd tell me if I did."

"Any weakness?"

She grunted. "Her weakness is her strength— she's *too* strong for the rest of us. Doesn't really fit in."

"Ever talk about men?"

She looked me over. "Like you?" she asked, looking at my chains. She laughed. "Coming to think of it, men might be more attractive if they were permanently chained. Because she gave me no indication she was ever attracted to the macho sex."

"How about you?"

"Hah! Men are animals," she said—"but women are worse, so there you are. I'm not exactly a man trap, physically or emotionally. And the guys around here?" she shook her head, "Pittsville."

"Know her mother?"

"Not much. Seems a little aloof. Like she's too good for the rest of us."

"How did she get here? I mean isn't this the elite of the outfit?"

"Morgan can do anything he wants. In a way, I think Suzanne is Dawn's chain. I don't think Dawn wants her around, looking over her shoulder. Criticizing...controlling." Irene leaned over to whisper in my ear: "To make matters worse, mother and daughter have lined up with the different factions. Dawn is with Neeley—Suzanne with Savage."

"How about you?"

"Me? Why do you think I'm in here? They're all a bunch of dorks."

Later that night the beans took their revenge. It was times like that when one wished for the saving grace of a skunk attack.

There were a couple of army cots in our cell—the stay might be longer than I'd hoped. Irene's showed signs of some use.

Sleeping on them was no piece of cheese, I can tell you, with the chains weighing down on top of you if you slept on your back. That, coupled with the hyperactive adrenaline and the revenge of the legumes kept me awake most of the night.

The next day I was visited by Savage and Neeley, contenders for the throne of J. Kent Morgan. They intensified their pressure on me and I stepped up my insistence on seeing the big man.

Savage asked me how I got on with my cellmate.

When I said, "Fine," he asked me what the whispering was about.

"Oh, not much," I said. "She hopes you will take over if anything happens to Mr. Morgan."

He looked at me as though he were the victim of a crude con.

I didn't react, but added, "Thinks you'd be the stronger leader."

The flattery hit the mark. It always does.

After Neeley put me through similar hoops and I ladled out similar flattery, he told me Morgan would see me on the morrow.

When I was returned to my cell, Irene was gone.

16

The offer to meet with J. Kent Morgan; head-man, was a believe-it-when-I-see-it kind of thing. All logic seemed to mitigate against it.

I spent the night alone and was surprised at how much I missed my cellmate Irene. I couldn't help but speculate on what had happened to her, and could only hope the solution to her irreverent nonsubordination was not terminal. And if she had been disposed of in that manner, what were my chances to fare better?

I still didn't believe it when the next morning I was unceremoniously hauled out of my cell by a lackey who deposited me in a car for the half mile trek. There was no loosening of the chains, and I was developing calluses where they continually abraded my skin when I moved.

We pulled up in front of the largest mobile home I'd ever seen. There were two of them hooked together, side by side. I hobbled to the door with the lackey's hand guiding me from its position under my upper arm. He knocked respectfully on the door and in a moment it was opened by Dawn, Lajos Bohem's daughter, who looked like anything but a captive.

If Dawn's demeanor was any indication I was in for a frosty freeze time.

"Follow me," was as warm and friendly as it got from Dawn.

I followed through a living room that bespoke great savings on interior decorator fees. I passed through a bedroom that looked like it housed a couple of cadets. A nice arrangement for the old captain, I thought.

Dawn knocked gingerly on the door and I heard a faux gruff "come in" from within.

Dawn opened the door and I struggled through it with my chains clanging, exaggerating my burden just a tad. I needn't have bothered, the subject of my ploy wasn't even looking at me, but far off in a distance that didn't exist in reality.

"Mr. Morgan," Dawn said, "this is Gil Yates."

He turned in my direction. There was a smirk on his platypus lips like you might find down at the pool hall on a guy who had just hustled you. A guy who looked like he didn't have the strength to lift the cue. His clothes, denim pants, a powder blue button down dress shirt and bolo tie did not display much of a fit, bespeaking a loss of weight since they had been custom made. The sallow complexion of his face was topped by an amateur brown dye job, probably self-inflicted so no one would know. Self-delusion is one of the saviors of mankind.

He did not appear to be in robust health. He looked like he had been deposited in the chair that reclined and jiggled when you were in the mood to jiggle.

I don't know why at that moment Morgan looked like a low end, discount store shoe salesman who would go for a smoke on his break, kick the stones under his feet and talk disappointingly about the local high school football team. Notwithstanding his plebeian looks, J. Kent Morgan had parlayed a window of self-confidence to the moon.

There was a king sized bed against the far wall— a desk and chair against a perpendicular wall. The furnishings looked as if they belonged to some well-off cowboy with an eye for bargains.

J. Kent Morgan was appraising me with the eye of a retired jeweler, no longer adept at appraising fine diamonds due to recently blurred vision.

He waved an insouciant arm at a chair across from him, and I deposited myself and my chains therein.

Dawn bowed out of the room.

"You FBI?" were the first words out of his mouth. His voice was high and scratchy.

I sucked in my courage, the twerp who labored under the fat thumb of Daddybucks Wemple, Realtor Ass. would not cut any cheese with Techsci's big cheese. "If I were, do you think I'd tell you?"

He nodded with his rheumy eyes half closed. "So who are you and what do you want?"

In a situation like this you have to decide quickly on which serves your purpose better, deception or candor.

"My name is Gil Yates. I'm a private investigator. My assignment was to find Dawn and Suzanne Bohem."

His eyes narrowed—could it have been in reluctant admiration?

"How did you get in here?"

"Sorry, my sources are confidential."

"And who gave you the map of the place we found in your pockets?"

"Ditto," I said. I had the uncomfortable feeling he was looking at my shoe—the one that hid the film.

"What were you taking pictures for?"

"My client. To document my—ah…success?"

His next question shocked me—so out of context was it: "How are you paid for your work?"

"Contingency. High fees—but nothing if I don't produce."

"Expenses?"

"I pay everything. Charging one hundred a day for expenses is tacky."

"How much would you get in this case?"

"One hundred thousand if I find them and document where they are. Your guards confiscated my camera and film before I could photograph them." One hundred percent candor wouldn't work in this circumstance. But why was he staring at my shoe?

"What do you know about Techsci?"

"Only what I've read—and been told."

"By whom?"

"Various people," I answered.

"What's your impression?"

"I must confess to harboring an opinion prejudiced by these chains"—I held them up meekly.

"Just a precaution," he said, waving my thoughts into insignificance. "We have a lot of enemies."

"What are you worried about?"

"Worried? You've no idea the forces allayed against us—the FBI, the CIA, the IRS. We've done a lot of good in the world—but you don't make omelets without breaking a few eggs. So we make enemies. They are out to destroy us—if we don't destroy them first. In this life it's eat or be eaten. What negative things have you heard?"

"Oh, that Techsci is a money-making scam. That you bilk people out of their life savings. That your simple homilies are fiendishly expensive."

"You think if they were cheap people would take them seriously?" He shook his head. "No, it is well known people only appreciate what they pay through the nose for. People like to brag about how much their psychiatrist costs them. Psychiatry—there's a scam. What do you want, really? And what are you willing to give for it?"

I don't know why I expected worse: a guy with horns and a forked tail? But Morgan was just a guy—worn out from a life of huckstering perhaps—who'd suffered from a surfeit of paranoia—only a little of it unfounded. They were out to get him, the only dispute is who *they* were.

"Let me take Dawn and Suzanne Bohem back to L.A. I'll split the fee with you. If they don't want to stay in L.A.—and I suspect they don't, I'll personally see that they come back."

"What's your fee if you get them back?"

"Two hundred thousand"—I could tell the number impressed him and my proposition was not rejected out of hand. "Fifty more if they stay in L.A.—don't come back here."

"How does one hundred fifty sound to you?

Our share."

"It sounds like more than half."

"But it would require groundbreaking exception to our rules."

"What rules?"

"People sign on here for life. They renounce the outside world. They don't go back. When they do, they become our enemies. They do whatever they can to tear us down."

"Well, they do complain you fleece them of all they have."

"We do not *fleece* anybody. What they give us is voluntary. In the Hindu religion, members give all they have to the faith. You don't hear anyone criticizing the Hindus for that."

The old guy seemed half asleep as he made his points.

"I suppose," I said slowly, "if you let them stay we could swing the one and a quarter."

"One fifty."

"Ah—you know I have considerable expenses—you don't want me to lose money, do you?"

"You know that movie maker," he said, ignoring me, "Lajos Bohem, who you want to reunite with his daughter, molested her?"

That astonished me. Could it be? I didn't want to believe it. Do human beings really do that kind of thing to their own? "How would you know that?"

"She told me," he said simply. "You want to give him another chance?"

I didn't know how to answer that, I thought he was lying. "You are quoted as saying lie, cheat, steal—

do anything you have to destroy your enemies. Is that true?"

"Basically they do all that and more to destroy us."

"You fight fire with fire?"

"That we do."

"But how do you account for all this conflict, this consternation—the Methodists don't have it—why do you?"

"People give us money—or the title to their property—quite willingly—whatever their motive, whether it is to get the plaudits of their fellows or out of completely altruistic motives. Then they have some disappointment. Human nature being what it is, disappointment is inevitable—they become disenchanted, and hell breaks loose."

"Ever think of just giving the money back?"

"Thought of it—but what a terrible precedent. Soon we'd have more people wanting their money back than we had money to give them."

"That many unhappy?"

"Course not. I'm just illustrating."

"So, what are your plans for me?"

"I don't know—what can you do for us?"

"Can't do much cooped up in chains."

"And if we let you out?"

"Well there's the one hundred twenty-five thousand for starters."

"One hundred fifty—"

"Well, whatever, it's all moot now, you have me gotten up like a mass murderer."

"Just a precaution."

"So you say. You know, there are people here

jockeying to take over the church. I wouldn't be surprised one of them might get overly anxious and try to hasten your demise." I checked his expression, it was passive. I had the suspicion the idea was not new to him. "Seems to me you could do a lot worse than having an objective private investigator looking into it for you."

There was the longest silence in the history of man—it was as though he were considering every angle as well as reliving his organization's history.

"How would you go about it?" he asked at last.

"Infiltrate. Pass me off as a convert. I'd offer to trade my allegiance—and willingness to stay here for freedom from the shackles. When I satisfy you on impending coups and what have you—you let me take the Bohems for a brief visit with the molester. I'll stay with them and see that they come back—if they want to. Even if they opt not to come back, you'll be one hundred twenty-five thousand richer."

"One hundred fifty thousand," he said.

I looked at him through a cocked and dubious eye.

"One hundred fifty thousand," I said.

17

The chains came off! I was a man unfettered. J.
Kent Morgan was a crafty old soul. And he had an eye
for the dollar. Lucky me. I could as easily have decayed
in my chain suit, and who would have missed me? Lajos
Bohem, but he'd miss my pseudonym. Dorcas a.k.a.
Tyranny Wrecks, but I wonder if she wouldn't simply
count her blessings and let it go at that. Daddybucks
would be irked initially at the inconvenience, but he
always said a secretary could do my job, and I think he
believed it. Who in these parts had ever heard of Malvin
Stark?

My children? It's a toss up.

I moved into my new room on the top floor of
the dormitory. Spartan flatters it. A bed, a wooden
chair and desk. That was it. The bathroom was down
the hall. My assignment was to do nothing. Go to
meals at the dining hall, if asked say I was a new convert, here at the sufferance of J. Kent Morgan himself.

I didn't have to wait too long. Savage was suave,
but he couldn't hide his *nervosa* from me. He had a little office in the multipurpose building and invited me
in for a chat after lunch. I thought he expected me to

refuse. But I followed him like a naïve lamb.

His digs did not inspire any awe in this bird. A cheap wooden desk—a chair on his side of it, two on mine. I decided those two chairs were a sign of exalted status.

When we sat in our chairs—his on the important side of the desk—he said, "I trust you have been made comfortable." There was something in his tone that told me he wanted me to believe he had been instrumental in my release and my newfound luxury.

I nodded noncommittally, not taking my eyes off his shifty orbs.

"Well, I'm glad you're out of those chains. Not my idea to chain you like an animal."

"What happened to Irene?" I asked while I had the opportunity.

"Oh, your cellmate? She was only fettered to teach her a lesson. She learned it."

"Is she still here?"

"I think she left."

"That's possible?"

"Certainly," he said, uncomfortable in his position. He was a man who asked questions, not answered them. "So you got to meet Mr. Morgan."

I just looked at Savage as though I had the upper hand.

"Get along all right, did you?"

I shrugged.

"Must have," he allowed, then as if to explain he waved a manicured hand in my direction. "No more chains."

That's very observant, I thought, but decided I should know Savage better before I wise-mouthed him. The wrong word from him could get me back in the chain suit before I knew it.

"So," he continued, "it was Morgan who brought you aboard in the first place."

I cocked an eye at him—the less I said, the more inner agitation he displayed.

"Or was it Neeley? Or both?"

When I didn't answer, he said, "You know you'd be better off cooperating with me."

"How better off?" I asked, calling his bluff in my best tough-guy stance.

"You know," he said vaguely, trying to intimidate me to butter with his glare. "You know you can't have too many friends in here," he offered by way of a weak explanation. "The old man isn't getting any younger, and, in case you didn't notice, he is not long for this world."

"That's too bad," I said, as though I meant it.

"Yesss," he said, hissing to an ending. "And that brings us naturally to the subject of succession. Who will the old man favor when the chips are down?"

"Who does he favor now?"

"I think he favors me," he said, looking at me for confirmation.

"Lucky you," I said, failing to keep the sarcasm out of my voice. "Why do you think he favors you?"

"I'm more like him," he said. "Neeley I call mealy mouth. He's Mr. Nice Guy, and I don't have to tell you nice guys don't win ballgames. He goes way back with the captain—they had a friendship like I never did. But friendship doesn't equate to leadership."

I nodded—"And nice is irrelevant to ability or success."

"Correct!" he said with too much enthusiasm. All the while I was cogitating how to play his Iago. I was hoping given enough rope he would solve it for me. So my silences grew longer, and dare I say, more poignant.

It worked! "How do you...ah...charge for your services?"

"Investigation, you mean?"

He nodded ever so seriously. Terrance Savage was a serious man.

"Contingency," I said, remaining cogent. "Lot of money, but only if I produce."

Another serious nod. "What could you do for me?"

I acted surprised—shocked even that he would consider utilizing my services. "What would you want done?"

"Give me an insight on Morgan's thinking. You seem to have access."

"You don't?"

"Of course I do—but not to his thinking. No one knows what goes on in that fertile mind of his. Is he favoring Neeley at the moment, or me? Or any number of others, like his lawyer, his accountant?"

"A lawyer or accountant? To run the...enterprise?"

"Church," he corrected. "Religious institutions are exempt from taxation."

"Yes, of course...church," I agreed.

"It wouldn't surprise me if he turned it all over to Horace Bernheimer, his personal attorney."

"What," I said, "are you proposing?"

"Information. What are others doing to get in with Morgan? You get me information, I use that information to my advantage." He said in-for-ma-tion so often and so ar-tic-u-la-ted my head was swimming.

"Advantage?"

"Of course. If I inherit the kingdom, you share in the spoils."

A quick calculation told me what a nice idea this was. It didn't take a Mafia Don to realize he could play both ends against the hindmost. If there were two main contenders, and I made them both the same promise I would be, as gamblers say, covering my bets.

"I, ah," I began speaking while my mind was still in neutral, "usually have a safeguard or two where my fee is concerned."

"What's that?"

"My fees, being so large and all, are dependent on the outcome of my investigations, which are often a matter of interpretation. So...I usually get the money in escrow with pretty specific instructions on its release."

"You don't trust me?" he said this with such a sense of moral outrage I was taken aback.

"I trust you implicitly. Who was it said, 'Trust the dealer but cut the cards?' Or 'Trust not your own father?' I don't know if those are Bible quotes or Shakespeare, but whatever, I've found it to be sound advice. Would you disagree? I mean, do you trust everybody?"

"Certainly not. I make judgments on the character of the person. Some people I'd trust. I'd have to trust you for example, not to divulge any of this to anyone."

"Of course I wouldn't. Confidentiality is the main tenet of my work. Once I've made an agreement that is satisfactory to both parties."

He gave me the red snapper eye. "Oh, so you're saying if we don't make a deal satisfactory to you, you are at liberty to repeat this conversation?"

"Who would I repeat it to? Morgan? He might not take kindly to my even discussing the matter with you after he has hired me to do his bidding."

"Neeley."

"Why would I?"

"Leverage? Get a better offer. Work both ends against the middle."

That was it: middle—work both ends against the middle, not the hindmost as previously reported. I swear I don't know how people can remember so many clichés so perfectly.

We haggled a while longer, then got down to the bucks and sense of the thing, and I was pleasantly surprised as to the depth and breadth of his pocketbook. Of course he was counting on getting his fingers on the pulse of the bank teller and being the one to control the flow of lucre.

Unhappily, he balked at putting anything in writing. "Too incriminating," he said. "Too many possibilities for leaks—for blackmail." He shook his head sternly. "'Fraid you'll have to trust me."

In the pig's pancreas, I thought. But it didn't take me long to realize I had the leverage of a one-legged soccer player. I had little to lose humoring him—besides, anything I put in writing would come back to haunt my house.

I could always wait for a better deal from Vic Neeley, whom I knew would inevitably contact me.

18

How wrong can you be? Let me count the ways.
I figured Vic Neeley would sidle up to me in twenty-
four hours and make his pitch. I was off by twenty-
three hours, fifty-five minutes and change.

I was walking from the tête-à-tête with Mr.
Savage to my room when I felt a large, warm hand on
my shoulder. I turned to face the ubiquitous grin of Vic
Neeley.

"How's it going, Pal?" he asked.

"Peachy," I said.

"Got a minute?"

"Nothing but," I said, intending to dazzle him
with my repartee. I don't think he got it.

He invited me to his office for a chat. His office
was the sneezing image of Savage's. It was as though
the great father of Techsci had decreed all his children
would be equal in status and no signs to the contrary
would be allowed.

"The old captain's fearful trip is about done, I
fear," Vic started as though he were drawing me into a
reverie he was having for some time.

His tongue tip showed through his lips, then disappeared as he pursed them. "That's one great man—" he shook his head. "Guess my expectation he'd live forever is not going to be met." He shifted his weight and looked out the window on a bright, benign sun.

"We go *way* back," he said, the reverie creeping over him like a slow growing moss. "Had some rough times. Lot of misunderstandings with the authorities. Had to take diversionary action for some years a while back. The old captain still isn't comfortable in public— why we're here when you get right down to it. It's always been a struggle, even after he made it so big."

"What exactly is he hiding from?" I asked.

Vic Neeley attempted to dismiss the notion with a wave of his hand. "Pettiness," he said, "government shenanigans. All tied up in trying to disallow our religion status—taxes, you know."

"What's wrong with him, exactly?" I asked.

The hand waved at me again. This time a hand of mystery. "Complications," he said, shaking his head.

I wondered who was making the complications.

"His mind is muddled," he said, "he forgets things. His promises aren't worth anything."

"Well, he promised to get me out of those infernal chains and, guess what?" I said, holding up my wrists for inspection.

Vic Neeley smiled. "You have me to thank for that," he said with a sheepish droop to his eyelids. "I keep his promises," he said. "I care for him."

"Am I going to get out of here?"

"Oh," he said, studying my face, "I suppose that could be arranged—in due time."

"What is due time?"

"When things get settled."

"Things? Settled?"

His head ducked like a sage, struggling not to appear superior. "You know," he said as affably as a backslapper at the Rotary Club—"when we settle the succession."

"Oh, I see," I said, without seeing that much— "you or Savage."

He nodded, and I imagined a touch of respect in the gesture. "I'm your friend—don't forget. I stand by my friends who stood by me. Next time you're with the captain, remember that. I can't say the same for Mister Savage. He's got lots of good qualities—he's Techsci down to the bone. The organization comes first with him. I'm more of a people person."

I loved that expression. People person. Since all persons were people and vice versa, I didn't catch the drift. But, it was my turn to nod, so I did.

"Now, a nice young fella like you could do a lot worse than to bet on this horse. You do, and I don't care if I win, place or show, you'll be taken care of. And, as I say," he added with a sly wink, "I can't vouch for Mr. Savage under the circumstances."

"Well," I said, cultivating the hayseed in me, "my priority is to get out of here—with Dawn and Suzanne Bohem. J. Kent Morgan and I made a deal."

"What kind of deal?"

"An exchange, you might call it."

"What do *you* exchange?"

"Money."

"Oh. Must be sizeable."

"It is."

"Mind telling me how much?"

"Yes."

He waited. "Well...how much?"

"I mind," I said.

"Hmm," he said, frowning. "Okay then, but tell me something," he leaned toward me. "Off the record. What did Savage offer you?"

"Offer me?"

"You know—to boost his stock with the boss."

I wanted to laugh out loud but held my larynx. I held his gaze in mine only as long as I could suppress my riotous explosion.

"About half," I said.

"Half? Half of what?"

"Of what you're going to give me."

19

Dawn and her mother, Suzanne, opted to talk to me on the move. We went for a walk. "No bugs," Dawn said, then asked me to pull up my shirt so she could see I wasn't wired.

As soon as we started down the path toward the mansion under construction, it became apparent Dawn was intent on showing me how fast she could walk. It was as though she were trying to get away from me and all I boded.

Suzanne held back. That was her way of resisting, so I was forever trying to shrink the extremes to get my audience.

A bird was chirping like a cell phone—one of those evenly spaced quasimusical rings—completing nature's never-ending quest for modernization: *Deus ex machina.*

In light of the outdoors, the contrast between mother and daughter was more startling. Suzanne still held a high percentage of her youthful beauty—with the chiseled features of the world of cinema and modeling.

Dawn, alas, had inherited her father's looks, and

those looks, awkward as they were on a man, were devastating on a woman. She looked almost androgynous. I had expected all of Morgan's cadets to look like Suzanne in her heyday. The fact that Dawn was Morgan's trusted aide certainly bespoke some inner beauty.

I laid out my plan in such a fashion I thought I would appeal to these two devotees of J. Kent Morgan. "Your loving husband," I looked at Suzanne, "and father"—I turned to Dawn who was steps ahead—"has offered to pay handsomely to see you again."

"Ha!" Suzanne spat. "You're only talking about the cheapest man who ever walked the face of this earth. And a world class swindler. Trust me, you have an agreement with him, he'll find some way to do you out of it. Can we slow down? My knees are killing me."

"I have it in writing," I offered meekly.

"All the better—Lajos thrives on the challenge. Better still it is notarized in front of the whole Supreme Court. Believe me, Lajos will find a loophole, and he'll drive his Humvee through it."

"The money is already in escrow."

She laughed. It was a laugh non-conversant with music. "That's one of his staples," she said, "putting the money in escrow. Hey, you're talking to his prime patsy. Didn't he put money in escrow for me before we were married?"

"He did?" Now I was having more serious doubts. "What happened to it?"

"He reneged, of course."

"Is the money still in escrow then?"

"Oh, no. He got it out."

"Without your approval?"

"Of course he had to have my signature."

"And you gave it to him?"

"I had no option. He said he'd divorce me."

"That's an option."

She shook her head. "Not then. I was pregnant. I didn't have the backbone to be a single mother and fight him for support. He'd have spent twelve million dollars to keep from giving me a thousand. It's just his nature."

I looked to Dawn up ahead for confirmation. She turned her head briefly, closed her eyes and nodded.

"Well," I said, "he can't divorce me."

"No, but he'll find *something*," she said. "Believe me, this is not a guy you want to work for."

"And not a guy either of us has any desire to see again," Dawn said.

I was fast approaching the end of my wit. Every plan seemed to be exploding before my eyes, ears, nose and throat. I looked around the bleak road, and said, "Don't you ever want to get into civilization again? Doesn't this brown earth get to you after a while?"

Dawn shrugged. "When the option is Lajos Bohem, this is the garden of Eden."

A biblical reference! So much the antithesis of Techsci, an organization that didn't believe there ever was a Jesus. I was not, however, confident enough to point that out to *mater* and *filia*.

"But..." I was less sure with every word I uttered, "...you don't even have to talk to him. All we need is for him to see you. He claims he just wants the peace of mind of knowing you're safe."

"Ha!" Suzanne said first.

"And double *ha!*" Dawn added.

"But, where's the harm?" I asked.

"Harm?" Dawn turned back on me now with the most terrifying look in her eyes. "I'll *tell* you where's the harm. That lovely man you say wants to be sure we're safe, molested me when I was twelve. After that I slept with a butcher knife under my pillow. I don't suppose you can relate to that—or maybe you don't care, but I'm not setting eyes on that creep again—not for one million dollars."

I gave a pleading look at Suzanne. Her eyes were downcast, but she knew I wanted some confirmation. She nodded, barely—pinching her eyes tighter.

"But," I spattered, "But...the money? The one hundred fifty g's for the cause. Wouldn't you do it for that?"

"You'll never get it."

"That's *my* problem," I said. "I'll get it," I added with more confidence than I felt.

"I'm not going," said Dawn.

"Neither am I," Suzanne added.

I looked over the brown, desolate landscape and thought how perfectly it matched my mood. Hopeless. I was stuck in these godforsaken doldrums and if I couldn't please the head honcho—I wasn't going anywhere—except maybe back in my chains. Since the money was the only spark of interest in him, I couldn't produce enough with the pictures I was carrying around in the sole of my shoe to pay him off, let alone have something left for my trouble, which was becoming more considerable with every passing moment.

Would he force them to go? Could he? I envisioned our trip where they both crawled out a ladies room window somewhere, never to be heard from again.

The coda of that opera was me rotting in chains in the Techsci tank.

We arrived at the mansion-under-construction in silence. No one was working so we toured the project, and I was startled at the contrast with my dorm room, Morgan's trailer, and this opulent building—where all the finish decisions seemed to have been made based on price: the highest.

While we stared in silence at the extravagance, not to say waste, I posited: "Ladies, what is it about Techsci that appeals to you?" I waved my arm around the kitchen that had two of everything—refrigerators, dishwashers, double sinks, ranging ovens. "Is it this?"

"Freedom," Dawn said.

"Escape," Suzanne said simultaneously.

I played what I thought of as my trump card—Dawn's bartender love in L.A. "Sophie misses you."

Dawn flinched, but that was all.

On the way back I turned on all my persuasive charm.

It was like talking to Tyranny Rex.

20

Not wishing to take my meager chances selling J. Kent Morgan on letting me out, I decided that night instead of going to dinner, I would head toward the gate. Maybe luck would be with me and they would simply wave me through. What I would do then without a car, miles from nowheresville I didn't know. But out was better than in—I'd hitchhike and hope that the car that eventually picked me up would not have a Techsci for a driver.

Then, before dinner, sitting in my room in the dormitory, I realized no one would walk outside the gate. The road went only one direction, which meant I'd have to be picked up by a Techsci to get anywhere at all, and the traffic from Techscis was painfully sparse.

I made up my mind, I would have to "borrow" a car. But how was I going to do that in a place with so few cars?

I could wait until Leon came back—*if* he came back—and crawl in the tool chest for my prepaid return trip.

Then I had a stroke of genius. I went downstairs

to the room Dawn shared with her mother. I knocked—Dawn opened the door. Her mother was lying on the bed with a hot water bottled on her forehead.

"Hi," I said with good cheer. "How are you?"

"Miserable," she said.

Dawn said, "We're not going," and started to shut the door—an action which I easily blocked with an adroitly placed foot.

"May I come in?"

"Look," Dawn said, "I don't wish to be rude, but we aren't going—you won't change our minds."

A groan from the bed gave me hope. I looked at Suzanne in her misery and back at Dawn who was standing defiantly in front of me, blocking my ingress.

"I accept you are not going, that's what I want to talk about."

Dawn looked surprised. "What part of no don't you understand?"

I surprised myself by easing around Dawn and staking my claim to a square foot of the living space apportioned to the faithful. There is a saying three is very crowded or something like that—whatever it is, it's true. I crossed to the desk, where I sat on top of it, leaving the chair for Dawn should she so desire. She didn't.

"I took this job on good faith," I began. "It hasn't worked out, what with the chains, the dungeon, and your disinclination to cooperate in the face of your leader's desire you do so. Where does that leave me? Hi and sherry."

"Excuse me?" Dawn was perplexed. "What's that supposed to mean?"

"It's an expression. Don't you know it? An idiom"—I didn't dare say cliché for I knew what I did to clichés—"it means stranded—hi and sherry—or is it high *on* sherry?"

Dawn began to giggle—her prostrate mother, in spite of her efforts to play the suffering damsel, broke into the most raucous belly laughs.

Dawn caught her breath before her mother. "Dry—that's high and *dry*," she said. "Dry as sherry," and she guffawed some more.

"Whatever," I said as though they were making a mountain out of a gopher hole. "I've got to get out of here," I said. "You were my ticket, you withdrew, leaving me—high ho silver."

They were so amused.

"You have, I believe, access to a car?"

"I drive the Techsci car sometimes," she said, "get supplies and such—I have that access because Morgan trusts me—a trust I am not about to break."

"No, no, certainly not." I protested a touch too loudly. "You love it here—to each his own—but I think your mother needs help."

"Mother's fine," she said. "She was an *actress*— she dramatizes each sneeze as though she were doing a Shakespearean death scene."

"I do *not*," Suzanne protested.

"Anyway, I'd like to take her to a doctor. After he sees her, I'll vamoose—she can drive the car back herself."

"You're crazy," Dawn said. "You'd never get beyond the gate. A two year old could see through your harebrained scheme—and where will that leave me?"

"High and dry," Suzanne offered, and they never seemed to tire of laughing. I know they were making fun of me, but it diverted their minds from more incriminating matters.

"No can do," Dawn said. "Sorry, I'm not getting myself busted to give you the car key."

"No, no," I said, holding up my hand. "I don't want you to *give* it to me—I'll take it from your room when you're at dinner. Or Suzanne can bring it. She really *needs* a doctor."

"We don't believe in doctors for little stuff around here. To save a life, okay—surgery, fine, but not for headaches. Morgan would never approve. That's what Techsci is all about anyway—dumping your rubbish so you don't get these psychosomatic illnesses."

"It is *not* psychosomatic," Suzanne protested, shifting the hot water bottle on her head just a tad.

"So just leave the key in the drawer—I'll come in when you're at dinner—I'll coerce Suzanne into going—to save her life. They won't dare stop us at the gate with that story."

"Wanna bet?" Dawn said. I was not winning her over.

"I'm not going," Suzanne said with a quiet, even dignified, defiance. "Too risky—you might be able to handle the chain treatment—I'm not. Besides, how do I know you wouldn't just drive me back to my husband to collect your fat reward?"

"You have my word on that."

"Oh *really?*" Dawn squealed, and Suzanne burst out laughing again. "Your *word*, huh? That's *fantastic!*" she said when Suzanne calmed down, "Thanks anyway."

"Okay, I'll go it alone."

"And steal our car?"

"I'll leave it in Santa Ynez—in the parking lot of the market."

"No thanks," Dawn said.

"I'll hide some Tylenol in the car—Suzanne can get it when no one's looking."

"God, you're naïve."

"All right—look. You don't want to go back to Lajos Bohem—and I can't blame you. But I've got to go back and tell him. You know how he is—another day without a report to him and he'll put out an all-points bulletin on me. And one of these days the feds may just bust in this place and haul away J. Kent Morgan for the final time. You want that on your head?"

There was an encouraging silence. Dawn broke it—"I'll ask him," she said.

I sighed a weary almost hopeless sigh, befitting my manifold burdens. Then I shook my head—"Won't do. Present him with a *fait d'accompli,* and he'll thank me for keeping the feds off his back. Tell him first and his paranoia will kick in and he'll be paralyzed into inactivity. I'll still be here—and you have to admit my presence doesn't serve any legitimate purpose—Suzanne will still be sick and Lajos Bohem, a.k.a. Uriah Heep, will go on the warpath."

"And our lives will be infinitely less complicated. Impossible," Suzanne said. "And no matter what, that old Ford pickup parked in the lot behind the dining room will be a red flag at the gate—especially with you in the driver's seat. I don't know how you'd ever explain how you entered my room while we were at

143

dinner and plucked the key from my middle desk drawer. You may say you were only borrowing it, but it's going to look an awful lot like you stole it."

"I don't think it's worth the risk. I'd say your chances of getting out successfully are slim to none. I would strongly advise against it," Dawn said moving to the door.

"Me too," Suzanne said struggling to her feet. "The biggest bottle of Tylenol you can buy—and a jumbo Advil. Put it under the passenger seat."

I nodded and I think my admiration was showing.

They stood at the door—"Now out," Dawn said. "I don't want it to seem like I'm *giving* you the key. Come back in ten minutes. Wait till everyone's at dinner."

"And remember," Suzanne said, "we strongly advise against it. I wouldn't give a nickel for your chances of ever getting out."

Dawn followed Suzanne out and waited in the hall for me to follow. I did. Dawn closed the door without locking it.

21

My exit from the Techsci compound was going to require a solid plan of attack. I would have to be more convincing than ever before.

There's no denying I would have been more comfortable with Suzanne in the car—an emergency medical guest. But it was not to be.

I tried and discarded many plans of action. Not convincing, stretching credulity, something was wrong with each of them. I even considered ramming the gate but I didn't have the confidence the truck could break the chains and still be operable.

I wish I could say I had a real good plan for getting out, but I had to take my opportunity before time ran out. So I made my way to the Bohems' room, took the key and sauntered to the parking lot, attempting to look guiltless. I don't have any idea that I succeeded, but I didn't see anyone notice me.

You can't start a pickup silently, so I tried to do it as quickly as possible. It was not to be. There was a lot of huffing and puffing, and, dare I say, cursing before the engine engaged. Again luck seemed with me, and I drove on down the road to the first guard house, which was blessedly unattended. I would consider that too much good fortune to stand. I allowed myself the luxury of fantasizing how I would dismantle the gate, should there be no one there to open it—or to stop me, as the case may be.

As I approached the main gate, I saw the guard with the automatic rifle strapped on his shoulder. If the goal was intimidation, he succeeded.

I was going to be nonchalant. I pulled up to the kiosk slowly, and respectfully. I rolled down the window. "Hi, how's it going?"

The fella with the Uzi didn't share my good humor. He was, conversely, downright dour.

"What can I do for you?" he asked with a hand on the stock of the firearm.

"Let me out," I said employing my nonchalant arrow.

"Got permission?"

I chuckled. "I'm on a medicine run for the big man himself."

The look of awe I'd envisioned didn't materialize. "Name?" he asked.

"Gil Yates."

He wrote it down. My heart was ding donging my rib cage. I willed him with my vision, to open the gate. He got on the phone instead.

He seemed to stay on the phone forever, and with each passing eternity I saw my chances of escape sink out of sight.

I felt the headlights on the back of my neck

before I saw them in the rearview mirror. Their car pulled so close to the pickup as to touch the bumper. Two swell fellas bounded out of the car and approached my front windows, like officers of the law making the standard safety approach to a suspect.

In the spirit of cooperation I rolled the window down again. "Hi, fellas," I said, cheerful as all outdoors.

"Get out of the car with your hands up," the role model said.

I obliged them. They were not long on chit chat, and I accepted their invitation to accompany them back to the heart of things where, to my surprise, they deposited me in the presence of the big man himself, J. Kent Morgan.

He was shaking his head and clucking his tongue in the act of communicating solid disapproval of my actions.

"Why?" he asked. "That's all, just why?"

"Suzanne needed some medicine—"

"Didn't want to ask permission?"

"It never occurred to me—I'm not used to being anywhere where you can't come and go at will."

He nodded, but not in agreement, rather in a kind of acceptance of my lame brain. "You told the guard you were getting it for me"—the head shook again. "You don't even know we don't put much stock in medicine here—should have tried something else."

"Well," I said, disingenuous, "I thought you'd have more clout at the gate than Suzanne. It was a harmless try, that's all," I said.

That infuriating nod burrowed in on me.

"Around here," he said, "we value the old fashioned virtues like loyalty, honesty, reliability. Did we, or did we not, have a deal?"

"I fully intend to keep it—"

"Then why were you running away in a stolen vehicle?"

"Borrowed," I corrected him. "I had some things I had to attend to."

He shook his head sadly. "I'm afraid I don't have the luxury of endless time. I'm on my way out. I just don't want anyone to hasten it. Divine providence has put you in our midst. You may be my savior."

The way he looked at me I got the queasy feeling he meant that literally.

"Oh, I don't know that I could be of any help..." I dissembled.

His nod told me he'd put that in the malarkey bin. "The likes of Lajos Bohem hires you, you can't be any piker."

"Why don't you let me fulfill my agreement with him—collect your one hundred fifty grand."

He closed one eye, and looked at me through the other. "Very nice," he said in a surly tone that indicated the opposite. "I had in mind a reverse order. Help me, *then* the trip south. You go south first, I wouldn't expect you to return."

I looked at him with a slant eye of my own. "You don't really mean you think someone might kill you?"

"Oh, no?"

"Aren't you the big boss here?"

"That's the theory, but physically I'm not the

big anything anymore."

"So why would you have anyone here who might want to harm you?"

"Oh, listen," he said, "you don't know. I've built this colossus—from the dust of the ground like God in Genesis. I want to perpetuate it—go on forever. Can't do that without a strong successor—can't do it without a well-liked successor either. So I got both—but they are different people. The strong one isn't well-liked—the well-liked one's not strong." He shrugged his meaty shoulders. "What can you do?"

"And you think one of those would kill you to be the last one standing?"

"Stranger things have happened."

"So what do you want from me?"

"Find out if one of them wants to, shall we say, hasten my demise."

"How am I going to do that?"

"You're the detective. Use your expertise."

"Well, short of asking them..."

"No, no, no. Something like that is going to require a lot of collusion. There's the doctor—the lawyer—both have to be corrupted. The lawyer has to get me to sign the will appropriate to their cause."

"What about the doctor?"

"He has to certify the death—the cause—let the local authorities know I wanted no autopsy—against my religion," he said, smiling broadly, "and I wanted to be cremated right away and my ashes scattered at sea..."

"True?"

He shrugged. "What *is* truth? Stalin or was it

Lenin? Said truth was whatever served the cause of communism. Here it is whatever serves my successors interests. Do I want an autopsy? Not really. I don't want anyone poking around my body. It's so unseemly somehow. But if there was hanky panky? Ditto cremation. You do it right away and dump those ashes out of reach of the labs"—he spread out his hands.

"Geez," I said, "what a mess."

"Now you know what they mean when they say it's lonely at the top."

"Okay—but by your own admission it would take a lot of collusion, and in a place this small I don't see that happening without some friends of yours hearing it. What makes you think your lawyer and doctor would both turn on you? Haven't they been loyal for some years?"

"Yes—but money talks, and believe me—there is a lot of it to be had."

"But isn't it for the work of the 'church'?

"Oh, yes—ideally that's so. But the flesh is weak."

"Okay—so my point is, let me take the Bohems tomorrow. I'll be back with them tomorrow night."

He took a long breath. Then shook his head once. "'Fraid I can't spare Dawn just now. You might be surprised at how few people I can really trust."

"Suzanne?"

He waved the idea off. "She gives me a pain where I can't reach it."

"Why's that?"

"Suzanne is a hypochondriac. Everything we do is poised against illness caused by psychological baggage. She's the porter for the baggage. Saunas, release therapy—nothing works with her."

"Why do you have her here?"

"Dawn—her daughter. She's okay—I need her. The ma is for the birds. You can take *her* back and *dump* her—But *you* come back."

"Tomorrow?"

"Why not—?"

"Okay—but—one hundred fifty-thousand dollars—I won't get that much for returning Suzanne. Bohem really wants Dawn."

"All right—tomorrow Suzanne—bring her back here, and next day you can do the trick with Dawn."

It sounded good to me. Suzanne didn't want to stay in L.A. anyway. I could test Bohem's veracity with the lesser of his goals—his wife. If I got my payment for Suzanne and the film in my shoe, I'd promise him Dawn—for the final payment. That was the one I expected him to try to do me out of.

"How much will you get for showing him Suzanne?"

"Much less. I have to read the contract again. Less than half."

"Okay—sixty percent for me—whatever you get—and show me the contract."

"I don't have it with me."

"I understand that. Bring it when you come back."

I readily agreed, for I had no thought of returning.

"Now, of course," Morgan added, "I trust you like my own mother. But one can't be too careful these days, so, as I told you before, I'll be sending two of our best guards with you—just to see no harm comes to you, and of course to see that you fulfill your obligations here. The guards have the wherewithal to restrain you should that become necessary."

Perish the thought, I thought, but I only smiled a smile that would have been the envy of Lajos Bohem had he been here to see it. Tomorrow I would try one on him.

22

The next morning we piled in the Techsci car—
an oversized Ford—and pointed the radiator south.
There were four of us. Suzanne, who came kicking and
screaming all the way—she'd developed *becoup* symp-
toms the night before: lower back pain, a sinus
headache, a reprise of an arthritis flare-up. She complained so much I longed for the day she would catch
Alzheimer's so she would forget what was bothering
her. My wallet was given back to me. My camera was
not.

The two guards were something else. The older
one—perhaps in his late fifties, had not outgrown his
testosterone. Phil Culp was his name, and his lot in life
was to not let his underling—twenty-something
Zachary McCrumb—forget who was boss. Zachary had
his quota of testosterone, but he despaired of ever
putting it to proper use. Both were heavily armed—just
in case I got any untoward ideas.

Phil drove, I was in front, Zachary was in back
with Suzanne. I suppose that seating was arrived at after

considering all the angles of security and likelihood of an uprising.

As we pulled out of the parking lot in the big Ford, I looked out the window and wondered if I'd be able to give the goons the slip. It wouldn't be easy, but I would be ever vigilant for an opportunity.

You couldn't look at this landscape and not think how this desolation of the earth must spill over into the souls and spirit of men. I should have been sympathetic to Phil and Zachary for putting up with it in the service of their bizarre cause. The sense here was not of *joi de vivre,* but of dragging the garbage out of your consciousness and replacing it with any substantial joyousness.

I detected through their body language my jailers were relieved to get off the base for a spell, though they would not dare admit it.

We cleared the gates with an ease I could only envy. But before we reached civilization we were in for more miles of somber brown earth thirsting for a spot of rain to encourage the vegetation. It was lonely out there centrally located in nowhere.

Suzanne started right away complaining about her insalubrious health. Phil tried to quiet her down.

"Now Suzanne, we don't want to listen to that for the whole trip."

"Hey, this outing isn't my idea. I was *forced* to do it."

"It's going to help the club," Zachary said from the rear.

"How'd you get into this, Zachary?" I asked.

"Natural born," he said. "My parents are Techscis."

"Enjoy your work?" I asked, turning to look at him.

He shrugged. "It's okay."

"Have training in the use of those firearms?" I asked.

"Well, sure, what do you think?"

"What kind of training?"

"Target practice, stuff like that."

"What stuff?"

"You know."

"I don't. Do they tell you who to shoot and who not to shoot?"

"It's a judgment thing. We don't go shooting just for sport. Somebody's got to be in jeopardy."

"And you make that decision?"

"Well, yeah—the guy with the gun's got to decide."

Scary, I thought.

"How about you, Phil?" I asked the driver. "How'd you come to Techsci?"

"Off the street," he said. "Was in a dead end job, a dead marriage—I saw this palace with pretty girls that turned out to be a Techsci headquarters. Got tested and four years later—released."

"Like going to college," I said.

"We like to think so," he said.

"Ever shoot anyone?"

"In 'Nam," he said—"not here."

"Is Zachary right about deciding when to shoot?"

"It's common sense," Phil said.

One said self-defense, the other said common

sense. Which would I rather have point the gun at me? When I made my break, would that be common sense? Or even self-defense? I could, after all, marshal a posse of sheriffs to hunt them down—unless I was cut down in "self-defense."

Just in case I couldn't get away, I decided to ask about their takes on the political situation, back at the base.

"How do you like working for J. Kent Morgan?" I began.

"Really great," Zachary said. "Fine," Phil said at the same time.

"Who's it going to be when he's gone?"

"I don't even like to think about it," Zachary said.

"He's got some time left," Phil said, keeping his eyes on the road.

"But wouldn't it be a good idea to think about transition?"

"There's a staff—and a hierarchy. It will be fine."

"Hope so," Zachary muttered.

"You're less sure?" I asked, turning to the back seat.

"He's sure," Phil cut in, without any discernable happiness in his voice.

"Notice any jockeying for position among the contenders?"

"You always have that," Phil said—"any organization—I don't care what it is."

"Good thing, is it?"

"Good, bad—just *is*."

"You get any pleasure from your work?"

Phil seemed to jump in his driver's seat. When he settled down, he said, "Yeah, sure. It's a worthwhile cause."

"What is?"

"Techsci."

"How so?"

"The goal," he said. Did he seem to be faltering?

"The goal?" I prodded. "What goal?"

"Make the world a better place. Give meaning to our lives—release us from our bondage to self-doubt. Cut out the garbage."

"Techsci does that?"

"You bet. I been at it almost thirty years now. Not quite the ground floor, but I'm a trusted part of the organization now."

"I can see that," I said, not meaning any sarcasm—but I could see by his face he wasn't sure. "How long you been out in this godforsaken desert?"

"A while," he said.

"Ever get tired of it? Island fever, you know—"

"You get used to it," he said. "You can get used to anything."

"Is that one of the articles of your faith?"

"Could be," he said. "Why don't you start on the path of full release and see for yourself?"

"Hear it's pretty expensive."

"There are ways—working is one—you can pay"—he spoke with an eerie mystery that I didn't want to challenge.

I turned back—"How about you, Zachary—you ever long for a life in the real world?"

It took him long enough to answer that I knew what his answer would be, and also what he was thinking—which was not what he answered.

"Nah," he said. "I'm fine."

When we got to civilization I said I wanted to call Lajos Bohem, Suzanne's husband, to make sure he was available to see us.

There was some argument between the guards on the necessity, then the logistics. Phil would accompany me with a concealed weapon (illegal, but effective).

Of course, all the movies notwithstanding, I didn't think Phil would shoot me in broad daylight if I went up to a policeman and sought asylum. But simple escape was fraught with difficulty, as they say down at the dog pound. I might escape, but I could kiss goodbye my fee because I wouldn't be able to produce the B girls (all right, *women*) for that maestro of schlockmeisters, Lajos Bohem. I'd already dumped ten g's and change in my pursuit of the Grail most holy and I wasn't a guy who liked to give up when he was in a hole.

Phil made the decision to stop at a gas station so I could call Lajos Bohem. The message was clear. The phone booth was secluded enough so he could get off a clean shot should I try any funny business. He could get back in the car, and since no one else knew where I was or where I was from, it would be a cinch to escape detection.

Any notion I entertained of being left in the care of Zachary, whom I pegged for the weaker sister, was squelched when Phil got out of the car with me.

Bohem's secretary answered. I asked to speak to him.

"Who's calling?"

I told her.

"I'm afraid he's unavailable," she said. It always makes me wonder why they can't tell you he is unavailable *before* you tell them who you are. It would build more confidence in their veracity.

"Would he have been available to a different caller?" I asked.

"No," she said, suddenly trading voices with Jack Frost. "He's out of the office."

"When will he come back to the office?"

"I don't know."

"Can you reach him?"

"Is this an emergency?"

"You bet it is," I said. "You tell him I am delivering the goods. Very reluctant goods—so he must see for himself *today*. I'll come to his office unless he instructs otherwise. You got that?"

"Yes," Jack Frost answered.

"I'll call again in an hour or so. Reach him by then in case he wants to change the venue, or has changed his mind about the goods. I can always return them, but emphasize this is his one and only chance."

The booth door was open—Phil was listening to every word. It was not the time to signal my predicament to Bohem's secretary, so I hung up like a good boy and climbed back into the car.

23

We pulled off the 101 freeway at Topanga
Canyon to find another isolated phone booth for a sec-
ond chaperoned phone call to Lajos Bohem in the
Culver City MGM studios .

The great schlockmeister came on the line with
gratifying speed.

"Soo, Mr. Yaytz, you haf someting for me?"

"I do indeed," I said with a fine vigor to fore-
stall his walking all over me, which was his nature. "I
will be expecting the appropriate payment on delivery."

"What do you haf?"

"No more schmoozing. We will be there inside
of an hour."

"Where are you?"

"Will you be there?"

"I haf a busy day—I weel do my best. If you can
be more specific. Is tis worth my while?"

"It's worth your while. Call the escrow company
and alert them I'll want to pick up the check today."

"Today? What is your hurry?"

"This is a one day excursion."

"*One day!?* You expect me to deprogram my girls in one day? Impossible!"

"Shall I turn around?"

"Be reasonable."

"I leave the reason to you. I am hired for a specific purpose which I am fulfilling, so I expect to be paid, promptly—and in full for agreed upon service. Now I've got to go. Please alert the escrow company"—and I hung up amid his protest. I rolled my eyes at Phil. It behooved me for him to think we were pals.

There on the asphalt of the gas station I shared some of my plan with Phil. He made macho noises of protest, but I reminded him J. Kent Morgan's edict was not to interfere with my plans, but to see that Suzanne and I were returned to the base safely. I would, I told Phil, be bringing money, so Phil was to be especially vigilant about my safe and prompt return.

The next two stops were a camera store and the escrow company.

We didn't readily find a camera shop, so we ducked into a chain drugstore, where I bought a Polaroid camera, and a three pack of film.

Back in the car, I formulated my plan in the general silence, only interrupted by the intermittent laments from Suzanne about her chronic aches, pains and general discomfort. I thought of dissing her about not knowing what discomfort was, her not being chained as I was, but I thought better of it. There was no percentage in making an enemy of her.

We rolled into the escrow company parking lot in Beverly Hills. It was Bohem's idea we use one of the tinier escrows—he was not a man to be seen in some funky, down home escrow in Culver City and environs.

Ms. Hippelfinger, the escrow officer assigned to our affair, was somewhere between buxom and frump, and I suspected, though she gave no overt evidence of it, that she envied the shape and relative youth of Suzanne.

We lined up in Ms. Hippelfinger's office and Phil did the honors with the Polaroid—three of them just to be sure. Ms. Hippelfinger was holding the date in front of her erstwhile bosom and Suzanne was the only one of the three of us who didn't feel compelled to plaster a phony smile on her kisser.

I asked Ms. Hippelfinger for the requisite check, and she said what I knew she would: "Under the terms of the escrow, Mr. Bohem must give his written approval of any disbursement."

"But you've seen I've produced my end of the bargain."

She shook her head. "I don't know that. This could be anyone. He has to be satisfied."

There was the rubber, of course. In spite of my best efforts, Bohem could find a passel of ways to weasel out of the deal. I could keep him from getting his money out of escrow since I'd have to agree to returning it to him, but he could, by the same subway ticket, keep me from being paid. I had no illusions he wouldn't avail himself of every opportunity to stiff me. After all, I was recommended to him by the biggest stiffer walking, Michael Hadaad. I should have known better than to get tied up with anyone who even knew the name Hadaad.

The closer we got to Suzanne's husband, the more she complained of her sundry illnesses.

"I don't think I can go through with it," she sniffed.

"Buck up, Suzanne," I said, "it's for the cause. This will make you one of Morgan's favorites—overnight."

"Think it will put me on par with my daughter?" she asked, childlike.

"I'm sure of it," I said.

The entry to MGM Culver City was nothing special. It was a neighborhood with aspirations to be middle class. Somehow I had hoped for a faux Roman coliseum or at least a fair imitation of the Appian Way.

We parked on the lot in a special space given as a perk to Lajos Bohem in appreciation of all the filthy lucre he caused to be lavished on the studio with his flicks that testified to the visceral hold he had on the nine year-old mentality.

As soon as Bohem's secretary—a single woman in her forties with a dollop of dishwater in her hair—buzzed him on the intercom, he came flying out of his office like a lead stuntman in one of his potboilers.

"Suzanne!" he shouted like a Shakespearean ham playing to the stalls, and threw his arms around her without seeming to notice how she cringed and tried to withdraw. "It's so *good* to see you again—come in—come in," he said, dragging her into his office and ignoring the rest of us.

Phil and I exchanged glances. He made a start to go after them. I stopped him with a wave of my hand.

"She's not going anywhere," I said. "We're on the third floor"—I turned to Bohem's secretary—"Are there any other doors out of his office?"

I could tell she wasn't sure she should answer—"He has a private entry from the hall—but only uses that rarely."

"Like now," Phil said, and darted to the hall. In a moment he was back—"This the door?" he asked the secretary pointing to the next door in the hall—a half block down.

"Yes," she said, and I hoped she was telling the truth.

"Zachary—get down there—yell if they come out."

We cooled our arches for an eternity. Well, perhaps fifteen minutes, but Phil was getting buggy—like he had insects in his pants. "What's going on?" he demanded of the poor secretary who was decidedly, loopwise, out of it.

The voices from within crescendoed like the percussion section in the eighteen-twelve overture, when finally Suzanne came storming out of the office screaming, "I can't take any more of this. Get me back home!"

Lajos followed her to the waiting area presided over by his secretary. "Now, Sweet Meat," he said and the words sounded bizarrely anachronistic coming from this Hungarian mogul, "listen to *reason* for once in your life. I weel get you help. I weel save you from tose predators."

Phil looked down the hall and waved Zachary back—If they were predators, he must have reasoned, two predators would be better than one.

I walked into Lajos's office and beckoned with a silent command for him to follow. No one was more surprised than I when he did. But so I wouldn't get the wrong idea about who was in charge, he said, "Tis is totally unacceptable."

"Oh?" I asked. "What is?"

"She weel not listen to reason. Tose people are taking advantage of a defenseless woman in a depressed state."

I nodded in agreement, then said, "Not my problem."

"What do you mean? How can it not be your problem? You are my representation with tose vultures."

"No such thing," I said. "I was hired to find your wife and Dawn, and I found them. I have fulfilled part of the contract and I am demanding payment."

"I don't see Dawn," he said. "Where is she?"

"Do you have the digital flash card reader I sent your secretary? I want to show you I found your daughter."

"Why did you not bring her?"

"She wouldn't come. But I haven't given up. I can say with some assurance that when I get Suzanne back Dawn will come."

"Tat would be good. But not for two hours. I haf to haf her for a week, at least."

"That might be nice—but that is your problem. I have fulfilled my contract by merely bringing the women to you. It is your powers of persuasion that must take over from there."

"But tat is not tah spirit of the contract."

"Spirit? I don't deal in ghosts. I knew you'd give me flack—that's why I was so careful with the contract. Now, according to the contract, I am entitled to have one hundred thousand dollars released from escrow."

"Where do you get tat?"

"Get me the reader and I'll show you."

His face reflected his utter disgust in me. I suspect he knew he was in a corner and would have to make forceful but illogical arguments—and difficult as that may seem there was no one better at it. He called his secretary to bring in the digital film reader to hook up to the computer. Then, almost as an afterthought, he drew out a pistol and pointed it at my head. "Or would tis be better?" he asked with a rather menacing smile.

"Better for what?" I asked, overcareful of my grammar under stress.

I hope he got the message as I sat and crossed one leg over the thigh that I wasn't scared. It was the message I hoped to send, though not an accurate portrayal of my feelings. I was scared out of my liver.

I took off my shoe and popped the film out of its secret compartment. I looked back at Lajos, and his gun.

"Lajos, you want me to show you this, or do you want to shoot me to save the fee? Might have a hard time making it look like a suicide. Tsk, tsk," I clicked the roof of my mouth with my tongue, "Think of all the budding adolescents who would be deprived of your cinematic genius if they put you in the slammer and threw away the key."

He waved the pistol at me as if to say, You don't scare me—though how I could scare him when he had the gun was beyond my imagination. But he put it back in the drawer and mumbled, "Just so you know I haf it—no funny business."

Bohem's secretary brought in the reader, hooked it up to one of the great producer's computers, and was kind enough to bring the image to the screen.

Lajos looked at the screen: "My baby," he muttered with emotion too low to be recorded on the Richter scale. "You must bring her to me."

"And I will," I said—"as soon as I get payment for this delivery."

"Well, but it weel take some time."

I shook my head. "Don't have time. I have to get Suzanne back before I bring Dawn. I have to have the money before I take Suzanne back. I have already been to the escrow company to alert them you would be releasing partial payment. I had Suzanne photographed with me there—I brought a copy for you." I took the Polaroid out of my pocket and handed it to him across the desk. He frowned at it.

"'Tis proves nuting," he said, but he knew it did. "My main interest was in securing my dear Dawn—Suzanne is veery dear to me, but Dawn is only a child and I feel a great responsibility."

I wondered if he felt anything like that when he molested her, but the introduction of topics like that in this situation could prove counterproductive.

"The situation is simple. You want Dawn, you pay for Suzanne as agreed."

"Yes, yes, I weel pay—*after* I see Dawn."

"You've seen her pictures. That triggers a payment."

"Where did you find tem?"

"Not part of the contract. Ask them. They want to tell you anything, it's okay with me. Confidentiality cuts both ways."

"But I am paying you?"

"I'm relieved to hear that. So you will fax your approval of the payment to the escrow and I will pick up the check on the way out."

I could see his mind working. Could he get them to give me a check they could, and would, stop payment on?

"I weel see. I cannot promise."

"There is nothing to promise. I have fulfilled that part of the contract and I will do nothing else unless I am paid as agreed. You may think about it. It will take us twenty minutes or so to get back to the escrow. If there is no check—and in the full agreed upon amount—there will be no Dawn. I will cancel our agreement and take you to court for payment. I can imagine the papers will get a big kick out of a guy as rich as you reneging on an iron clad agreement with a wuss like me."

He looked at me with the eyes of a cinematographer lining up a climactic shot. "No agreement is iron clad," he said with a melodramatic menace.

24

We headed back to the escrow company. I can't say I was sanguine about the check being there. I expected a long, hard battle—but in the end, if he wanted the goods...I thought it would be like the contract negotiations: stumbling rocks every step of the way, but a final capitulation. But as they say, the proof of the pudding was very likely to be somewhere in the pudding itself.

Ms. Hippelfinger, our fearless escrow agent, was on the phone, so the four of us cooled our extremities in the posh waiting room. Phil was getting impatient. So was I. Zachary looked like he was content with his lot, it being not too challenging for a young fella in his particular predicament.

Suzanne thought she was catching the flu. "These closed, windowless spaces are death. You can catch simply *every*thing through the air conditioning ducts."

I clocked the wait at twenty-six minutes, and I expected Ms. Hippelfinger would have been falling all over herself apologizing for the delay. Instead we were ushered into her office where she told us, with a certain engaging want of ceremony, "That was Lajos Bohem on the phone. Says he's not paying until you complete the contract."

I nodded. I wish I could have feigned surprise. "You have the contract. You know that several steps have been completed. I brought him his wife, and I showed him photos with his daughter indicating I'd found them. Check the papers."

Ms. Hippelfinger shook her head. "When there's a dispute, it's between the parties. If you get him to direct me to pay you all the money, I'll do just that. He says you didn't produce his wife *or* daughter, you waved them in front of him and took them away. He had no chance to reason with either."

"If it was reason he wanted, he should have stipulated that—Lord knows he stipulated everything else."

"And he says you refuse to tell him where you found them."

"Ditto," I said. "They don't want him to know."

She threw up her hands. "My hands are tied," she said, contradicting her show that they weren't tied at all.

"Let me call him," I said.

"Wait a minute," Phil said, "We'd better be on the road."

"No," I said, "your boss will not be happy if we return without the lucre. It was the deal."

"You know you're not going to change his mind," Suzanne said. "And I'm not willing to spend another five minutes with him for any amount of money."

I picked up the phone on Hippelfinger's desk without asking.

"Dial," I said, not displaying the joy I'd hoped she would at the action. What did she care? She had control of the money and could extract her fee like an oral surgeon.

When Bohem's secretary answered, I said, "Put him on—"

"Is this Mr. Yates?"

"How did you guess?"

"Your innate charm can't be disguised," she said, and the click of the hold button met my ear.

I wasn't sure who would come back on the line—the secretary to say the mogul was not available, or Uriah Heep, the creep, himself.

I got lucky—maybe—the big schlump himself picked up and met my bombast with the oil of reason.

"Look here, Yaytz, at least one of us has got to be reasonable and it looks like it has to be me—by default. I am not going to pay you one hundred tousand dollars without reasonable time to talk reason to my loved ones."

"The *contract*," I interjected.

"Tah *spirit* of tah contract," he countered.

"The *letter* of the contract. Any court will uphold my position, if you want to travel that route."

"Courts are reasonable," he said, "and I don't crumble under threats. Now you bring me my women and *leave* tem with me for some time—"

"So you can have them deprogrammed?"

"Possibly," he said. "At least I need time to *reason*."

"But they don't want to do that," I said, yet again trying to get him to understand their feelings. "That was *not* a stipulation of our agreement."

"Well, but it was *understood!*"

"No. All I had to do for the first payment was find them. I found them—now you want to renege."

"I don't want to renege. Tell me *where* you found tem and I'll pay."

"Sorry," I said. "I'd do that if they'd agree. They don't agree."

"Well tat's jest stupid," he said; he was warming up now, the oil was starting to ooze out of him—"I'd pay you all tat money without knowing *where* you found them?"

"Read the contract—"

"But tat's *understood!*"

He seemed to have a lot of understanding at odds with mine.

"Come on," Phil said, "let's go. You're not making any headway."

"My head is killing me," Suzanne chimed in.

I'll say this for Bohem, he was in no hurry to get off the phone. That's when the horrible thought hit me.

I reiterated my intention to take the matter to court and hung up.

"You are wasting your time," Lajos had said, and I was much afraid he might be right. The court could side with him. My fees were on the high side, and who could tell how a judge would view them? And unless

Heep the Creep agreed with me in writing, he was not about to release one dime to me.

When we got outside my fears came to fruit. Across the entrance to the escrow company a car was parked. Inside it were two of the least savory fellas you ever saw. Against the three of us, arms and all—no contest. I'd already decided I should buzz the bug out of there and write the whole thing off as a bad experience—win a few, lose a few more kind of thing. When your *modus operandi* was contingency, you were bound to have a few losers. The trick was knowing when to bail the situation. In my humble judgment, that time was now.

Of course Phil had strict orders to bring me back and escape was not going to be easy—but with this new element of being followed, I might work something out.

We got in our car, I didn't say anything about my suspicion until I was sure.

Sure enough, we pulled away and they followed.

"Take a right at the corner," I said. "Drive around the block."

"Why would I do that?" Phil asked, not happy at my suggestion.

"I think we're being followed."

Phil looked in the rearview mirror and did what I'd suggested.

They followed us right back to where we started. That's why Lajos Bohem spent so much time on the phone with Ms. Hippelfinger and then with me—to get his goons in place. "Can you shake them?" I asked. It was obviously to my advantage to do so, for if Bohem found out where the girls were, I'd never see a penny.

"Try," Phil said, and began some fancy maneuvering with the car, but he was apparently outclassed by the pros who managed to stay with us uphill and down alley, in and out of parking lots, wherever we went, they followed.

"I have an idea," I said.

"What?" Phil asked.

"We split up, the four of us."

"No way."

"Take us to a hotel where taxis are lined up. Three of us hop out and take a taxi each, you drive the car. They won't know who to follow. Bohem probably told them to follow Suzanne, but we'll see."

"Cute," Phil said. "Real cute, but no cigar. You'd fly the coop so fast your head would spin."

"Oh, ye of little faith."

"We don't use that back in Techsci. Morgan doesn't believe there was a Jesus."

"How about you?"

Phil shrugged. "Doesn't cut any ice with me, one way or the other."

"So we'll split—two, one and one. I'll stay with Zachary, Suzanne and you go alone—the two who aren't followed can rendezvous somewhere and rent a car."

"You're crazy."

"Okay—you explain it to Morgan when we arrive in camp with those guys on our tail."

Phil was thinking. I got the feeling thinking was not his forte.

"I suppose you could always open fire on

them—depending how you feel about a nice chunk of time in the slammer."

Phil was frowning. "How about just the tires? You think you could hit a tire or two if we pulled along side?"

I turned to see Zachary grinning with pleasant expectations. "You bet," he said.

"I'll just slow down—" Phil said, "wave them up—they'll want to see what we have in mind—then you shoot the tires."

"Wait a minute," I said. "You think they're unarmed? What if they shoot back—higher than the tires? Not a pretty picture."

"That's a point," Phil said, and I'm embarrassed to relate I was buoyed by his approval.

"So, we split up?" Zachary said from the back seat.

"Can't be done," Phil said. "Too risky."

"Risk. Talk about risk," I said, flipping a glance at our pursuers. "For all intensive porpoises, we are cooked geese."

"*What?*" Suzanne asked and threw in a couple coughs, sneezes and wheezes for sound effects. "*Intensive porpoises?*" she started to laugh but it made her cough too much. "*Intents* and *purposes*," she corrected me. People love to correct you, have you noticed? "And the saying is our goose is cooked, not we are cooked geese."

"Oh, shut up," Phil assayed, showing the state of his nerves. He knew we had to do something, but didn't know which of the scant options would be more prudent.

"Let's analyze our situation," I said. "These guys want Suzanne, and they want to follow us to find her daughter, Dawn. That's why we have to split up—to confuse them—and that's why Phil has to stay with Suzanne—his superior judgment and experience in this stressful and highly dangerous situation are needed. I'll go back with Zachary—I've got a lot of money at stake, so you won't have to worry about me. We'll meet you somewhere with three cars and they'll be so confused they won't know fire from the harvest moon."

To show what he thought of that Phil ground the engine and tried to shake the goons behind us.

They weren't shaking.

25

We drove aimlessly in patterns that Phil thought were clever and evasive, but we still couldn't shake the goons.

"I have it!" I said. "Leave Suzanne off at a police station—I'll stay with you if you're worried about me escaping. The only chance at a fee I'll have in this nightmare is back at the ranch. The cops will keep the guys off our tail."

Phil frowned. "Suzanne might have to answer too many questions," he said.

"Yeah, well just think of the questions we'll have to answer if they kidnap Suzanne—that or you don't get back in one piece."

"I can take care of myself," he snapped.

I threw up my hands. I decided on a decidedly negative spin. "Okay—no skin off my pancreas, they nail us, I won't have to go back."

"Ha, you just said you *wanted* to go back! Think I'm a moron?"

I said, "I can't argue the proposition either way."

I spent the next hour in silence, hoping Phil

would eventually see the light. But after sixty minutes of speeding, two wheel corners and zigzag driving, the sweethearts were still on our tail.

I wanted to knock some sense into our leader's head. But in my experience, the man behind the gun was seldom known for his intellect.

"Still think you can shake them?" I asked anyway.

Phil made some animal sounds, and I was not surprised at how natural they sounded.

"You know," I said, folksy-like, "they want Suzanne—obviously. Not me, not you. They probably have orders to shoot at their discretion, and I wouldn't give a nickel for their discretion. They shoot, it's going to be *us,* not Suzanne. If we didn't have her as a shield, we'd probably be goners."

Phil's mindless peregrinations took us through Inglewood and Hawthorne, and it gave me an idea.

The airport.

"Phil," I said, "I don't want to doubt your expertise in ditching a shadow, but before you know it we're going to run out of gas."

He reflexively checked the gas gage.

"And when we do, and they pull up at the pump behind us, we'd better not have Suzanne in the car—or we better dig in for a shootout. Why don't you head for the airport—if we can't lose them there, we can confuse them."

Much as Phil hated to take orders from me, even his numb skull could absorb the sense of it. He turned the nose of the car west. He climbed to the ten freeway and our shadows were right behind us.

"Here's what we can do," I said. "Let Suzanne and someone off at Delta—she runs in and hits the tunnel for Skywest and gets a plane to Santa Barbara, where she calls Techsci for a pickup. You two guys block any attempt of the goons to follow her."

"And you?"

"I'll go with her," I said with a touch of proud chivalry in my tone.

"In a pig's ear," Phil said.

I'd given them the unacceptable alternative on purpose. If two went with her, I'd have an easier time of giving Phil the slip in the confusion of the airport.

"You up for going alone?" Phil asked Suzanne.

"Sure."

"We'll see they don't follow you—you should be able to lose *anyone* in this zoo in a couple of minutes—just hopping from one terminal to another. The three of us will keep the two of them from following you."

"Three?" I said. "Make that two. I'm not risking my life in this cause."

"You're not sitting in the car, either," Phil said.

"No? Why not? The place is crawling with police. Nobody is abandoning a car here—and nobody is getting inside with a gun."

"Time you come to realize you're not in charge here."

"Perhaps, but I don't think Morgan wants me to be a prisoner either. I'm working for him for crying out loud."

Zachary made a snorting sound from the back seat. "Anybody working for Morgan is a prisoner."

"Watch your mouth," Phil snapped.

"Say," I said, sharing my brain tornado, "don't you Techsciers have a God you can call on to deliver you from this evil?"

"We are all gods," Phil said.

"Great!" I said. "So put them in the fiery furnace."

"Idiot!" was Phil's retort. "Okay," he said, "here's what we're going to do—Zachary's gonna take Suzanne to the plane, I'm gonna let them off at the International terminal. Go to one of those shops and buy clothes and hats and sunglasses. Then hit the next terminal. Leave your gun in the car, Zachary—if one of them follows you, tell a cop. I'll do the same—work your way through the terminals until you get to Skywest. Get her a ticket to Santa Barbara and see she gets on the plane without one of the goons. Then call headquarters and tell them when Suzanne's arriving. Then work your way back to the International terminal and we'll pick you up."

My idea, but the international terminal was a nice twist. I wouldn't be looking for any credit.

Phil stopped the car at the Tom Bradley International terminal—Zachary and Suzanne jumped out. The goons pulled up—had a quick discussion and the passenger jumped out and followed Zachary and Suzanne into the building. It was a toss whether or not they had enough time to lose him. If he was as deft on foot as they were driving, I didn't have much hope for Suzanne. But my feelings were mixed. If they caught her and returned her to Bohem, I'd have an even greater claim on my fee.

Phil and I left the airport without being followed and we found a fast food greasy fork and settled in for overcooked hamburger and soggy fries. Shades of Daddybucks Wemple—only this time I was not paying.

26

Back at the airport there was no sign of Lajos Bohem's henchmen. There was also no sign of Zachary.

"How long we going to wait?" I asked, after ninety-some minutes.

"You got a better idea?" Phil snapped.

"Yeah, we go in there and look for him."

"And leave the car at the curb?" he asked with the full force of his sarcasm testifying to the low esteem he held for the idea.

"No—one of us drives around the airport in case Zachary got confused and wound up at the wrong terminal. Not, if I may say so, an impossible fish kettle."

"What?"

"What what?"

"Oh, I get it, fish kettle. You mean kettle of fish."

"Isn't that what I said?"

"Not quite."

Language, I always thought, was a matter of communication. If you were understood it didn't matter what words you used.

"Well," he said, after faking some intellectual exercise, "I'm not letting you alone. Strict orders not to."

"Suit yourself. We aren't getting anywhere with the buddy system—be honest with yourself for once—just the two of us—all I'd have to do to get away is step out of the car and go to some policeman or national guard kid and tell them you're armed. No, you wouldn't shoot me—you'd be a dead turkey in seconds, and shooting me could hardly be worth it."

"You don't think I'd get a fair trial and a suspended sentence?"

"No, and you don't either. Those kids in the camouflage suits are just itching to use those automatic rifles they lug around all day. I'll go one step further—you don't *have* to shoot me—just step out of the car with your gun—shazam! you don't even have to point it at anyone and you're a historical memory."

"History," he corrected me. "I'm history."

"I'm glad you agree," I said. "So you want me to check out the Skywest scene, or drive the car?"

He obviously didn't care for either alternative and didn't want the blame if anything went wrong, and something obviously had gone wrong. He dithered, and every minute was precious.

"So call J. Kent Morgan and ask his advice. He wants us to abandon them, I'll go back with you—voluntarily. Make sure Morgan knows that."

Phil frowned. I'd put him into an untenable position: I'd given him a reasonable suggestion without taking the time or trouble to make him think it was his idea.

The duty cop was approaching us at the terminal

curb—"Let's move on," I said—

"No Zachary?" he said, half a question half a statement of fact, precluding my suggestion.

"We'll circle. Look for him—then come back after you talk to the boss."

He didn't like the idea, but he didn't have a better one. The cop was waving us away from the curb with a National Guardsman in his camouflage fatigues covering his flanks, so Phil, with a show of reluctance, eased the idling car into the maddening traffic that was the Los Angeles International Airport, affectionately known as LAX.

He was fumbling with his cell phone—obviously not the latest or most expensive gadget of the genre when I offered—"You want me to drive?"

"I can do it," he said, letting me know he'd had about all the suggestions he could take from me.

"You don't think it's dangerous to drive and dial?"

Without answering, he pulled to the curb of another terminal and dialed. It couldn't have been more than a few seconds when the phone was picked up and Phil turned on his obsequious charm; Lajos Bohem could not have done better. He was obviously talking to the big taco himself. It was paining to have to report what sounded like an episode of the Keystone Kops, and I could see him flinching at every barked reaction to the thunderous put down coming through the cell phone. For an instant I marveled at how this conversation was shooting up to some orbiting hunk of something and shooting back for a trip of perhaps ten thousand miles to reach someone one hundred miles away—or across the street for that matter. Somehow the conversation did not seem worthy of all that travel.

I couldn't hear what J. Kent Morgan was saying, only feel the rumbling reverberations of his gravely displeasure.

A guardsman was approaching us with a wary expression. He waved us on. Phil nodded sweetly and pulled away from the curb to go with the traffic.

Phil handed me the phone. "Wants to talk to you."

I took it and gave a, "Hello," which aspired to be cheery but didn't come close.

"Yates?—What's going on there? You exposed us to a barrel of snakes. Now Zachary's missing and Suzanne could be too. What have you got to say for yourself?"

The old man was angry, no gainsaying that.

"I had no idea my client would act like a moron!"

"That's some consolation," Morgan said, heavy on the sarcasm. "I got the IRS and FBI and Federal Marshals closing in and I can assure you, I don't need this two-bit producer joining the hordes of heathens striving to bring us down."

I started to talk but he wasn't in the mood to listen.

"I *trusted* you," he bleated. "You were going to bring home the bacon—" he paused as though a new idea was crowding his brain. "You *did* get the money, didn't you?"

"Ah—" I fumbled.

"Oh, no," he said, getting the idea on his own.

"You certainly have turned out to be a disappointment, Yates. We'd have been better off keeping you in the chains. To think this charade had my approval."

"Yes, sir," I said meaning more contrition than agreement. "And, I take full responsibility for it. I was on my way back with Phil to help you out with your other problem, but I'm willing to call it quoits."

"Quoits? What are you talking about? Oh— quits—call it *quits?* Jump ship. Not bloody likely. Phil's instructions are to bring you back here directly. And you'd better have a good and believable explanation about why you're coming back emptyhanded. I intend to debrief you myself."

"And what if you don't like what I have to say?"

"We'll see—"

"Back in chains?"

"I hope not."

"Well, just a minute here," I said toughening up the delivery—"I'm going to need some pretty convincing assurances if I volunteer to come back there."

"Volunteer? It was a condition of the trip, remember? You were going to the end of the rainbow and bringing back the pot of gold. Money was a sure thing. In escrow, you said."

"It is—he just wouldn't agree to let it out yet—I haven't given up hope—but I think I might be more effective here."

"Out of the question!"

I paused long enough to have him say, "You still there, Yates?!"

"I'm here," I said, "but the larger point is, I don't have to be. You, I and Phil know I can walk out of here anytime I want."

"He's armed," Morgan said, and I think he realized how foolish that sounded.

"He's armed in the car. How important is it to you we find Zachary—and maybe Suzanne?"

"By God you better find him—Techsci is all on your head. Don't think for a minute you can get away from us."

"I *know* I can. All I do is walk. We are in an *airport* in 2002, remember? Kids with automatics all over the place. Phil isn't going to shoot me, and we all know it. I was coming back voluntarily—to help you with your own little problem—and coincidentally make a nice fee—but I'm not comfortable with the attitude. Lot simpler if I just bailed the ship as you suggested."

"I didn't..." he stopped.

Then, as though he were gently cinching his position, he said—"We have people all over the face of this planet, Yates—you can run, maybe, but you can't hide." He paused to let that sink in. "Yates," he said, his voice turning sad, "things are heating up here. I'm not *safe*. I can feel it. I need you here—your expertise, help me hold off the vultures. You can smoke out the plot, save my life—you can't let an old man down—so near the end." He paused, and I could hear his breathing. It sounded frightened. "So," he said, "what are you going to do?"

I took my time and listened to more breathing, which turned to wheezing. When I couldn't stand his agony any further, I said, "I'd like to help you, I just want to be assured if I come back I'll be safe there."

"You'll be safe."

It will go a lot easier if you tell Phil here to trust me—I am a private investigator—I've found dozens of missing persons," I exaggerated just a wee tad. "Tell him to consider me from now on, not a prisoner, but a comrade."

"Comrade?"

"Equal? Is that better?"

"Okay, put him on."

I handed the phone back to Phil. "Yes, sir," he said, and he yessed him a bunch more times, looking at me warily in the intervals. Finally he added a snappy, "Yes, sir, for Techsci!" and punched the button to turn off the cell phone.

He looked straight ahead in silence, and I could see he was trying to digest the disagreeable pap he had just been fed by his boss, and it was not going down easily.

Without looking at me, he said, "Okay, hotshot, where to?"

"The airport police station," I said.

27

I could tell Phil thought I was a genius when we found Zachary locked up in the police station. I didn't see any sign of Suzanne so I assumed she had gotten away while Zachary made a covering scene with the goon.

I didn't broadcast my hunch when we were directed to the holding tank where Zachary was reposing. His visible skin was sporting a good display of black and blue indentures, and at first glance it looked like someone had given a denture and a half to the cause.

The officer in charge—not a bad looking woman, who a generation ago might have been a pre-school teacher—was glad to see us. "Get him out of here—mixed it up real good with another bozo. Took 'em in to cool 'em off. Know these other two?" she said, pointing to our nemeses.

"Nah," I said.

"Apparently friendless," she said. "Tried to get bail but couldn't drum up any interest. I'd let them out if you could vouch for them."

The expression on their faces was worth the price of admission.

My face was blank. I looked at them as though they had terminal rabies "Sorry," I said, but wasn't.

"Tell Bohem to get us out of here."

"Bohem?" I said. "Make you a deal. He pays me what he owes me, *I'll* get you out."

"But..."

We were gone before he completed his thoughts, such as they were.

We waited until we got in the car in the parking lot before asking what happened. Such was our paranoia.

"The big one took after me and Suzanne. I told her to run for it, and I blocked him. Had a time of it, I'll say—keeping him down—oh, he did some damage I expect, but she got away."

"You don't know if Suzanne got on the plane?"

"No. I didn't get that far with her—but neither did he. Cops pounced on us—phew there must a been a hundred of 'em."

"At least," I muttered.

I could tell Phil was out of joint because I was the one that thought of the police station. It's always a good place to start, but I wouldn't expect a sheltered Techsci to know that. Mingled with that animosity was a sense of relaxation at his finally accepting that I wasn't going to run. Of course as the days dragged on, my cover with Tyranny Rex and Daddybucks was wearing thin.

The mood in the car was sullen. I think they resented that I had an in with the boss. "Been with him thirty some years," Phil muttered, and let it go at that and an uncomprehending shaking of the head.

It was after eleven when we got back to the Techsci ranch. The guard at the first gate told us J. Kent Morgan wanted to see me right away. "Thirty years," Phil grumbled, "and it's *you* he wants to see."

Phil drove me to Morgan's trailer, and though I was as tired as a dead man, I got myself out of that car and up to knock on the door.

Dawn answered. "Oh good," she said. "He wants to see you right away. I'm to wake him—let me get him up and I'll come back for you." She left the living room, and I felt took an inordinate amount of time. But she did come back with a weak, almost pitiful smile on her face. "He'll see you now," she said.

She ushered me into Morgan's bedroom, where I found him propped up on an acre of pillows, looking none too wonderful for the wear.

Pale and wan, he exerted a great effort to wave me to the chair pulled up beside him.

"I'll be in the kitchen if you need me, Mr. Morgan," Dawn said, and withdrew gracefully from the commodious bedroom.

Morgan looked at me and every gesture required an effort—even the eye movement. "You came," he said, a horse in his throat. He didn't have to tell me that pleasantly surprised him. "It's been grim around here," he said, then fell silent. It seemed as though he was deciding how much information he could trust me with.

I filled the silence with a candid, trust-me comment: "If you don't mind my saying so, sir, you are not looking well."

"You're telling me," he muttered.

"Has something happened?"

"That's what I want you to find out."

I frowned. How, I wondered, was I going to do that? "Hey you, you poisoning big taco?"—Not bloody likely.

"Theories?" I asked.

He rolled his eyes. "I can tell you, I don't feel good."

"Been to a doctor?"

"I have my own here."

"Competent?"

"I used to think so."

"Hmm—get a second opinion."

"Opinion? Based on what? I feel weak—not exactly rare at my age."

I nodded—"But you look ashen—"

"Yeah, like the reaper had scared the daylights out of me."

"How so?"

He licked his lips—"All paranoia is not unfounded."

"So what's going on?"

"Someone's trying to get rid of me. I've become a nuisance to the organization I founded." He bestirred himself to a dry laugh.

"Any ideas who?"

"Ideas? Who? Who not? The only person left who is unassailably loyal is Dawn. That's why I have her here."

"Couple of men wanted to off you, what good would she do?"

He thought, then shrugged. "Witness? Inhibiting factor?"

"Then they'd kill her too—"

He pursed his lips, then shook his head. "It's not going to be Gangbusters. This is a slow—poison-ing—kind of thing."

"But doesn't Dawn feed you?"

He nodded.

"And you trust her—"

"Implicitly."

"Medicine."

He nodded.

"Your doctor gets it—gives it to you?"

He nodded again.

"How many pills?"

"Lotta pills," he said, waving a weak hand.

"Injections?"

"Some—"

"What?"

He shrugged. "Vitamins—I don't know. I'm in his hands."

"And you trust him?"

He shrugged. "Used to. Now I trust only Dawn—and as sure as God made little green apples, if I leave my body mysteriously, they'll blame it on Dawn."

"But I don't understand. Surely there's enough for everybody here. Why would it be necessary to...do away with you prematurely?"

"Power," he said, his voice fairly booming under the shaky circumstances. "Which faction gets the power—the hand that rocks the cradle rules the world—"

I'd heard that expression, though I thought it more appropriate to say the hand that rocked the cradle ruled the nursery.

"So you think your doctor has joined one of the factions who want to do you in?"

He nodded, a weary fatalistic nod.

"What's in your will?"

He snorted. "Which will—mine or theirs?"

"You mean someone could have forged a will?"

"Not that hard to do."

"But who, and how—and why?"

"That's what I want you to find out."

"Any suggestions how I go about winning the confidence of someone who wants to murder you?"

"No one wants to murder me—they just want me dead. Natural causes would suffice. As to how you do it—that's your specialty, not mine."

"Can you tell me what was in *your* most recent will?"

He looked perplexed. "I've changed it so many times I have trouble remembering which version is last."

"Why change it so often?"

A wry smile came to his lips. "Keep 'em guessing. Keep 'em dancing to my tune. I love it." A frown replaced the smile. "Trouble is, their dancing is now fake. I can feel it."

"Where can I find your last will?"

"Oh, I suspect Dawn can produce it. You want to ask her?"

I stood up.

"You're a godsend here, buddy," he said. "I'm in no shape to pursue these demons myself."

I found Dawn in the kitchen washing dishes. I made my request, and she dried her hands and marched through the living room, the master's bedroom, into his office—that was the thing about trailers, not room for hallways.

I stayed in the bedroom with Morgan—returning to my bedside chair.

"You use a lawyer to write these wills?"

He nodded.

"Where does he hang out?"

"Here."

"Here? He lives in the compound?"

"Yes."

"The doctor too?"

He nodded.

"And they're competent—licensed members of their professions?"

He waved a dismissive hand. "Techsci has attracted high types throughout its history. You know, I started this..." he seemed to be groping for the right word..."religion," he said with an odd twist to the word and his lips. Was he about to acknowledge that calling his pop psychology a religion was a stretch?

He didn't seem inclined to go on, so I asked him in my most naïve fashion—"How did you decide to call it a religion?"

J. Kent Morgan stiffened on his pillow farm, then relaxed, as though he realized the fix he was in was not conducive to displays of pride, for as they must say in the legal profession, pride goeth before a slip and fall.

"Over forty years," he said, with a distant look in his eye that could have placed his heart and soul in that era, "I started this...thing...on a shoestring. I studied psychology—read a lot, and distilled the wisdom in the parlance of everyday common-man language. I wanted to help all these sad creatures of the planet to get on." He stared off into space as though he were considering making this a last rite of candor. "I wanted to help my fellow man—all mankind, actually, and I was inevitably part of mankind, so I was not completely devoid of self-interest. I wrote a book—"

"I read it—"

"Put it all down in black and white—caught on like wildfire. Made a lot of money. Paid a lot of taxes. Religions don't pay taxes. Religions fill a need. I was filling a need. Two and two makes four. We went religion—the bureaucrats wanted a god—we are all gods. They wanted worship service, we gave it to them—we had clergy in clerical collars. Just to show them how ridiculous it all was."

"Made some money, did you?" I asked, redundantly.

"Made some *real* money," he acknowledged.

"More if you don't pay taxes?"

"Much more. The taxman is a bloodsucker, little girl."

Little girl reminded me that Dawn seemed to be taking a long time locating the will. I considered commenting on that, but decided the question answered itself.

"What about these people who gave you their houses and whatnot who want their money back?"

"There are always beggars at the gate," he said. "They gave freely—we spent."

"Freely?"

"Sometimes—at any rate, we don't have their money to give it back," he said, and his eyes glazed over in confusion. "If you could get a fix on where that money is, and who is controlling it now, I'll make you a rich man."

"So if you had to pick the most likely culprit in this scheme who would it be?"

He opened his mouth to answer, then was seized with a coughing fit.

Dawn came into the room. "Mr. Morgan—the will is missing, I looked all over for it—somebody must have taken it."

If Morgan heard her, he made no sign. His hands were at his throat. Dawn and I stood by helpless as his head slumped to his chest and the choking stopped.

28

Dawn threw herself on the dead man and intermittently wailed and sobbed. She wasn't faking it. She'd
adored him.

It was her idea not to tell anyone until the next
day. I was disconcerted by the thought, but rationalized
it was her baby—her "religion" or psychology or whatever, and I'd better butt out.

The good news was with Morgan out of the
way, I was off the hook for the one hundred fifty thou.
What was more disconcerting was the avalanche of the
faithful an hour later with stories that didn't do the
laundry for me.

I'd decided to keep the vigil with Dawn. My
innate chivalry kept me from abandoning the damsel in
her distress to the wolves and inevitably impersonated
carrion birds. And I've always said, birds of a feather
very much tend to fly in packs.

Savage led the parade of sudden mourners followed by the doctor, the lawyer and a few others I
didn't recognize—Neeley was missing, and that sent a
red bull up the flagpole for me.

My question, unasked, was how did they know to come and mourn so soon after he died when no one had communicated with them?

Dawn didn't move from Morgan's body when the onslaught came in—I couldn't say she even knew they were there. There was some hubbub about her being hysterical and in need of a sedative when lo and behold a doctor produced a syringe as though he were a magician taking a quarter from behind some yokel's ear. In one blurring arc he pulled down Dawn's pants and stabbed the bare mound of flesh he exposed. She gave a little yell, then went limp.

"Hey!" I yelled—"What do you think you're doing?"

"She needed a sedative. Relax her. She's hysterical. Do her good to calm her down."

"Don't you think you should have gotten her permission?" I asked before I felt someone's arm around my neck in a choke-hold. I was vaguely aware of some fiddling with my pants and the unmistakable prick of a needle in my gluteus maximus, but that was all. My next consciousness was opening my eyes in a barren field.

My first recollection was my focus returning from a blur to one lone tree, bent over on one side as though reaching for eternal rest on the ground. The next thing I saw was the distant mountains. Even in my reduced state I could tell they were not close—I turned the other direction: ditto.

The challenge was getting to my feet. I was too groggy to achieve much, but I rolled over on my knees and pushed myself up until I was resting on my knees, my back more or less perpendicular to the ground.

That was the easy part. The attempt to get on my feet did not go smoothly, and I fell back to where discretion dictated I remain for an indeterminate while, whilst I attempted to rejuvenate myself with deep breathing and small muscular movements of my tingling limbs. I had no idea how long I'd been there, my best guess was only overnight. My senses turned eagerly to sounds of life around me. A car, a train, a plane, a bird—I'd have settled for a beetle, but there was *nothing*. Perhaps I *was* on the moon. Maybe Techsci was a supernatural outfit and that surprising injection they gave me transported me to the extraterrestrials. I wouldn't have been surprised if at any moment I'd feel a hand on my shoulder, turn to face a jovial, young J. Kent Morgan saying, "Hiya, buddy—not much of a place, is it? We could've done better—but this is just the beginning."

Then I wondered if it wasn't all a dream, or some kind of hallucination brought on by the drug they shot in my gluts.

In perhaps another half hour I was able to struggle groggily to my feet. Wherever I was, in a dream or reality, I wanted to get out. But which way was out? When my eyes finally focused, I saw I was in a desolate valley between two mountain ranges. If anybody was going to find me here it would have to be a mountain lion. I could only hope he wouldn't be too hungry.

I searched the earth for signs of how I got in. I reasoned if they got me in from somewhere I could get out the same way. What I didn't care to reason was they had the advantage of some sort of internal combustion engine and I was hoofing it. I'd read survival statistics, how long one could go without food and water, both times being diminished by the burning of calories resulting from exercise.

I started my journey over the parched, roadless ground, never seeming to get any closer to my goal.

I finally came to a place with a path which was fairly clear and my spirits bounced as I took to it. A half hour later I was beginning to despair of having it lead anywhere when suddenly I came upon an unmistakable dirt tire track—one way. I followed the tracks out until I came to a dirt road—gravel, ruts and rocks. That was the good news. The bad news was it went in two directions and I didn't know which went toward civilization and which might lead to an abandoned mine or oil well.

From the position of the sun during the day I could tell daylight was fading and the road went approximately East and West. Since I was probably still in California—heading towards the coast would be the best bet. Of course, were I in Arizona, the California coast would have been a long schlep.

I walked perhaps an hour on the dirt road before I heard some sounds of surface life. Though I couldn't be sure, I thought I heard the distant sound of an automobile or truck—whatever it was was okay with me. I stepped with a renewed vigor, though thirst was beginning to rear its homely head, and my stomach was starting to talk to me.

After perhaps an hour, another vehicle was heard in the distance, but obviously closer than the first. I was encouraged. Then I realized the hearings were over an hour apart and I wasn't headed for highway 101.

Here my memory begins to get fuzzy. I know I made it to a real road—and by real road I mean one covered with black asphalt. But I can't remember how long it took me—because lack of food and water was starting to take its toll booth, and I was woozy with weakness. I think night was upon us, and if I'd seen any light on any horizon I might have been disoriented. As it was, I was on a road on Mars—no traffic, no people, no buildings as far as the eye could see.

And there—*some*where—sometime while patiently waiting for a sign of life—I felt mine slipping from me. Somehow I realized all my strength had seeped out of me like a leaky oil tanker and any further movement on my part would not be prudent.

Then I blacked out.

29

"Where am I?" were my first words on waking to the face of an experienced looking nurse old enough to be my mother.

It was while she was telling me "the Santa Ynez Cottage Hospital" that I noticed the tubes entering my body. "What are these?"

"Oh, just some precautions—you were pretty low on fuel when they brought you in here."

"When was that?"

"This morning," she said, "about eight."

"Who brought me?"

"I don't know—someone found you by the side of the road in some desolate part of the country. How did you get there?"

"I walked," I said.

"You *walked*? From *where*?"

"Where they dumped me."

"Where was that?"

"I've no idea."

"Think we should call the police?" she asked.

"I wouldn't object."

She considered the proposition. "Perhaps I should wait a couple hours till you're up to it."

"I'm up to it," I insisted. "Hours could be costly."

I must have fallen back asleep because it seemed only minutes until two sheriff's deputies were standing at the foot of my bed looking askance at me as though I were some sort of criminal. I soon discovered why.

One of the sheriffs, who said his name was Deputy Trenton, looked like a deputy farm hand—sun-browned leathering skin stretched over a skull pointing toward retirement. The other, younger version of John Wayne was introduced as Deputy Ledbetter. He had the swagger, but not the heart of a gun toting Ranch hand. I was surprised when old man Trenton started talking tough to me—as though I were on the ten most wanted criminal list.

"What's the last thing you remember?" he asked.

"Waking up and seeing you at the foot of my bed."

"Don't get funny," he snapped, displaying what I thought was a rather ill-humor under the circumstances.

"I'm not trying to be funny. I must admit to being a bit out of sorts."

"Why?"

"Why?"

"I don't know what in sorts would be, so I don't know what out of them means."

"Physically," I explained, "I'm not with it. My body has been stretched beyond its capacity. I was dehydrated and undernourished."

"Why was that?"

"Because I found myself in a desolate area, and until I got myself to civilization my body was weakened beyond its ability to sustain me."

"Tell us why you were out there so far from anything," Ledbetter said kindly. The look on Trenton's face told me he didn't care for the competition.

"I was unconscious—so I can't tell you."

"Going back to my first questions—what's the last thing you remember—before you woke in that field?"

My mind went fuzzy. I scrunched my eyebrows. "I don't…" I started, then stopped, not knowing how to continue. What more to say? Pictures were swimming in and out of my memory, but they meant nothing to me. Deputy Trenton was looking at me funny-like—as though he didn't believe me. I really wanted to cooperate because I thought it would be to my benefit. Did I have amnesia?

"The field," Trenton prodded—"How did you get to the field?"

More fuzz. I pinched my eyes shut in the hope I could recall. I couldn't.

"Think!" Trenton badgered me. "Don't tell me you're pleading amnesia."

"Sheriff," I said, "I'm trying to remember. Believe me, I *want* to remember."

At that moment a young doctor strode into the room, having overheard our last exchange.

"Gentlemen," he said, "I'm going to ask you to leave the patient now. We'll try to get him back to normal. Leave your card at reception, we'll give you a call when he can talk."

It didn't take a seeing eye dog to grasp that deputy Trenton didn't care for that order, and he stood for a moment pondering how he could circumvent it. He was in a tough spot and he stared at the doctor for a long moment. The doc stared back at him and flashed a warm, if a trifle phony, bedside smile at the deputy and after gracing us all with another deep scowl, deputy Trenton huffed and puffed out of the room, dragging deputy Ledbetter behind him.

The doctor closed the door and returned to my bedside. He pulled up a chair and deposited himself on it like a bale of hay. He was a tall, thin sort, with hair care sacrificed to the exigencies of the job.

"Now," he began, "you can level with me—don't you remember about the field?"

"Waking up—" I said.

"But not how you got there?"

I tried again to remember—"I'm sure it will come to me in time," I said. "I just seem to have blanked it out—"

"Know where you live?"

"Well, yeah, sure," I said—"In California?"

"Good," he said. "Big place—California. Can you pin point it? Lompoc?"

"No."

"San Luis Obispo—Santa Maria, Paso Robles maybe?"

"No."

"L.A.?"

"That's more like it," I said. "Yeah—L.A. county—*Torrance!*"

"Good. How about your name?"

I started to say Malvin Stark, but caught myself

just in time. "Yates," I said—"Gil Yates."

He laughed. "Really? The *Rawhide* trail drover—"

"You've seen *Rawhide?*"

"When I was in high school I was a devotee of late night reruns—he said: Keep em movin', movin', movin'. Keep them doggies movin', *Rawhide!* Through wind and rain and weather, hell bent for leather, wishin' my gal was by my side..."

"Yeah," I said, my head clearing, "you know the words, that's really something."

"You named for Rowdy Yates and Gil Favor?"

"Don't know," I said. "I was so young at the time."

He smiled and patted my shoulder. "Well, how do you feel?"

"Okay—"

"Headache? Stomach bother you—weak?"

"No, I'm okay—"

"Good!" he said with a broad prairie smile. "So we'll keep feeding you through the tube for a couple more hours—and you get rested. You'll be good as new in no time." He rose to leave—"Try to get some more sleep—do you good."

Half way to the door, he turned back—"Oh, by the way," he said, "just out of curiosity, could you have deliberately lost your memory—conveniently—in front of the cops?"

I pondered and frowned. "I don't *think* so," I said.

206

30

I don't know how long it was until I realized what I really needed was a telephone. It was not too long after they took the tube out of my arm and my memory was seeping back into my head. I was a little frightened to think what too much police involvement would mean to me—I wasn't worried about the troops at Techsci, I was more than sure they could take care of themselves. Can you really be *more* than sure? I more than doubt it.

Later that day they checked me out—based largely on the fact that I told them I felt better than I did, and I would take it easy for a couple of days.

Just as I was released from the hospital and looking forward to a peaceful trip home—I had given up hope of wringing a dime out of anyone—I got as far as the reception desk where I was greeted by the craggy face of Deputy Trenton and the smooth peach fuzzy face of Deputy Ledbetter.

They invited me to come with them to the station. It was truly an offer I couldn't refuse.

When we arrived there—only a block or so from

the hospital—how convenient!—they sat me down in the interrogation room. No catering to the citizenry for them.

"So, have you got your memory back?"

"Pretty much," I said. "Though, I must add, I'm not convinced it's reliable—"

"Okay, start with the field. How did you get there?"

"I was out at one of your local cults, and some of the penitents overpowered me and gave me a shot which knocked me out—"

"Why would they do that?"

"Have to ask them, I guess. *I* wouldn't have done it."

"You a Techsci?" Ledbetter asked.

"No," I said.

Trenton was eager to retake the reins. "What were you doing there?"

"Private investigation."

Trenton bristled. "What kind?"

"Well, that's privileged with my client."

"Who's your client?"

"Ditto."

"Listen, don't get smart with me. You know P.I.'s don't have that kind of privilege. You know, J. Kent Morgan was murdered," Trenton said, his eyes glued to my face for a reaction.

I gave him one. "Murdered? No!...I knew he died—murdered—I don't believe it"—but even as I said that I knew I did. "Who done it?" I asked.

Trenton screwed his face to maximize the grim. "Insiders say Dawn Bohem...or you." His gaze never let up. Such is my naïvete that until that moment it had not occurred to me *I* might be a suspect.

"Oh, but that's ridiculous."

"Is it? Apparently you were both with him when he died. Yes or no?"

"Well, yes, but...listen, he was in bad shape. Pale, blue, weak. He'd been in bad health. What would have been *my* motive? I just met the man."

"There are a number of scenarios out there. Could have been a hit," he said, giving me the fisheye. "They say you fled the scene."

"I was dumped in a desert to die, and they say I fled? You can't believe that!"

He looked me over—"Well, maybe you were an accomplice."

"To whom?"

"Dawn," he said evenly.

"Dawn? More than preposterous! She was his staunchest friend."

"Not what we hear from the new leadership."

"Who's that?"

"Mr. Savage."

"Oh, my," I said. "Look no further—there's your culprit. Who had more to gain by Morgan's death—Savage...or me?"

He kept this eerie stare directed at my face. It was so disconcerting there were moments when I'd have traded those glassy eyed stares for the rubber hose treatment. "Let's talk about the facts. After examining Morgan's body, the medical examiner decided there may have been foul play. In this county, sheriff deputies are also deputy coroners, and I had to write up the report. Enough unfriendly drugs in him to floor an elephant. In my investigation the Techscis claimed Dawn

Bohem had the only access to Morgan, so we have to hold her."

"She's in jail?"

"Yes, and after you surfaced, Techsci said you were an accomplice. We've got to get some information from you."

I had a lot to think about, and I had heard enough. "Sheriff, I'm afraid I'm not up for much more—anyway could you take me to a hotel and let me rest another day? I'll be more than happy to help then—I'm just—out—of…"

"Sorts," Trenton said with a sneer. "Yeah, okay—"

They accommodatingly drove me to the Tess Barker Grand Hotel in Los Olivos, where they stood by me as I checked into a room on the second (and top) floor. Then they accompanied me there and left me with a stern warning not to flee and to call them as soon as I awoke. Deputy Ledbetter offered to stay in the lobby—anything to get away from Trenton, who chewed over the offer, then looked at me and said, "We'll see."

I settled in the cute country-homey room and wham! Tyranny Rex and Daddydandruff came to mind.

I don't know why, when I think of my beloved wife, Tyranny Rex, I start to get the shakes. Here I was rehearsing my story, paying particular attention to employing the truth in service of the lie—couching my narrative in phrases that simply mislead rather than intentionally deceived.

I was fairly trembling by the time I reached her on the phone. After I delivered my canned speech, which in retrospect must have sounded like gibberish,

Tyranny said, "That's nice."

Our differences have been irreconcilable for years—it's only perversity that glues us together. That and my palpable, if irrational, fear of losing my job with her father. The fear is grounded in what I consider my luck: to wit, if I didn't have the Wemple sinecure, my private investigation racket would dry up over night.

Her father, the august Elbert August Wemple, Realtor Ass., was not as easy a mark.

"Holy Toledo, Malvin, you sure are milking this little goldbricking to a fare-thee-well. What gives?"

"Getting rejuvenated," I said. "Need the rest."

"Rest? What do you *do* in your life besides *rest*? I don't know how long it's been since I saw you *awake* around here. You're the only bozo I know who can sleep standing up."

"Does your kindness know no bounds?"

"Kindness—you're right on the money, Malvin—if it weren't for my forbearance, you'd be in line at the Salvation Army soup kitchen."

There was no point in continuing that conversation, so I disconnected the phone line amid one of *my* sentences so Daddydandruff would think it was a bad connection. Fortunately he didn't know where I was and couldn't call me back. He could try the star sixty-nine trick, but would doubtless get the recording that said the call was out of the area.

I was so exhausted by the ordeal, I fell onto the bed and slept soundly for twelve hours.

When I awoke, my first thought was how to get out of this mess. Deputy Trenton seemed to have a gleam in his eye that said—"We're going to arrest you for murder."

I didn't see how he could do that—Techsci was not the first time I've been wrong.

When I got down to the lobby, I saw the headlines on a paper sprawled across a couch.

J. Kent Morgan Murdered
on Remote Ranch
Personal Assistant Held—

Dawn Bohem was arrested yesterday and taken into custody by the Santa Barbara County Sheriff's Department.

31

I zoomed back to my room, threw the deadbolt and fell back on the bed, staring at the ceiling, breathing too hard for comfort.

It was too easy to see the fix I was in. If Savage turned on her, he would turn on me. Did he know I was still alive? Or did he assume, more reasonably, that I had expired in no man's land and been eaten by turkey vultures?

Did the sheriffs tell Savage they'd found me? One could hope they'd be closed mouthed. On the other hand, my experience taught me that much hope was vain. Murder was the big crime—a plum for these bucolic lawmen. But their experience is limited—they don't exactly have the murder rate of New York City. They could have blurted my name. If so, the Techsci boys were sure to implicate me.

I called my voicemail and heard a lot of bombast from that mealy-mouthed client of mine. It all added up to his attempt, unsuccessful, to intimidate me.

When I calmed down and returned to rational

thought, I remembered my assignments—the chief of which was to try and at least recoup my too considerable expenses. I called him back.

"Okay, Bohem, here's the picture. Your nemesis has finally been disposed of."

"Good! He's dead ten?"

"Yes. I don't suppose it would do any good to remind you that triggers another payment."

"Did you keel him?" he asked with too much glee in his voice, hoping, I suppose, to hang a murder rap on me and get me out of his hair and his bank account. There was probably some law about not having to give a felon his money in an escrow account.

"No, I didn't kill him—but the bad news is they've jailed your daughter—"

"I saw tah papers." There was a long silence. "Murder," he muttered, turning the word on his tongue as though to see if it was at all palatable. Then he announced his decision: "Impossible!" I let that thought sink into his devious brain. "I want to help her."

"She doesn't want your help."

Silence. "Ten, well—weel she take your help?"

Nice—he was falling so beautifully in place— "You forget—I've been stiffed. I no longer work for you—"

"Now, Yaytz," he bleated, "don't be unreasonable—"

"Why not? You haven't been exactly the soul of reason yourself."

"Yaytz! Tis is no time to quibble with forgotten slights—"

"Sorry, Bohem, the grand financial slight—reneging on our agreement has not been forgotten by me. No further action on my part without you releasing the money that's due me from escrow."

Silence. "Tell me where you are and I weel send it."

"Sorry. You can send it to my bank in Torrance. If you're interested, I'll give you wiring information."

"I am interested."

"I'll call you back—"

"Oh, Yaytz—where is Suzanne?"

"I don't know. I suspect she's back at the Techsci compound, but this little charade puts a different slant on it. I couldn't guarantee anything." I paused for a delicious silence. "Get me the money, and we'll talk."

I hung up the phone, hoping he didn't have time to trace the call. Instead of a check from escrow, I'd be facing a couple heavies from one of his idiotic movies.

It didn't take much wallowing in self-pity before I realized I had to do something. I had to take the bull by the steering wheel and get out of there. First I had to recall my car rental, which was fortunately where I left it down the street from my hotel.

The good news was deputy Ledbetter was not in sight. Nor was anyone else I could identify as a law enforcer.

I drove to a gas station, where I used the phone to call Lajos Bohem with my banking info. He tried to pump me, but I wasn't pumping.

Next stop, the Santa Ynez Sheriff's station. I was

taking a chance on them throwing me in the slammer, but I couldn't sit by and let them frame Dawn for the murder.

I got lucky. Deputies Trenton and Ledbetter were off, and a nice-looking woman allowed as how she'd let me visit with Dawn, if she so desired.

She did, and we met in one of those impersonal four walled locales which would only be elevated in status by calling it a room.

Dawn was in reasonable fettle considering her fix.

"Do they really think you did this?" I asked.

"They're doing a good job of faking it if they don't," she said, slumping into her gun metal chair. "You get everybody agreeing, swearing to a lie, it can be pretty convincing. Especially when the cops are lazy and want to take the first explanation that comes along."

"But what kind of motive..."

"Oh, I don't think they thought that far. My fingerprints on everything."

"But they knocked you out—just like me."

"You too?"

"Yeah—I wound up in a desolate field. I suppose they left me for dead. I'm not eager to set them straight, should you have the opportunity."

"Okay."

"Have you got a lawyer?"

"Daddy had one of his stooges call."

"What did you tell the stooge?"

"I wasn't interested."

"Oh—well, I suppose there's a kind of nobility

in that stance, but you *are* in a fix. What are your options?"

"Truth?" she said it like she wasn't sure—and I don't blame her. "They're bound to see through those lies."

"I salute your optimism," I said.

"Why don't you tell the cops about the shot?"

"I told them," I said. "The bad guys will say you were hysterical and it was the doctor's considered opinion it would be best to calm you down."

Her blank eyes told me her untenable position was sinking in. Then she seemed to awaken from her bad dream. "You," she said. "You can help me. You're an investigator—investigate."

I started to tell her her father had stiffed me, but I thought better—didn't have much to do with the price of persimmons at this juncture.

"Yeah," I said. "Not much to go on. I don't expect a lot of cooperation from your jailers."

"Don't I have a right to counsel?"

"Sure do, but I'm not a lawyer."

"But if you're my choice..."

I shook my head. "Don't think it'll fly...but we can give it a go. I just don't want them throwing me in here for impersonating a lawyer." I sighed at my predicament. It looked like a loser all around. "Where's your mother?" I asked.

"They probably locked her up. Couldn't get her arrested by the authorities here so they probably took it into their own hands."

"Someone needs to investigate that compound."

"Amen," she said.

"What have they got on you, besides the finger-prints?"

"They claim I gave him something—not poison exactly, but something that reacted with his other medicine and stuff that caused his heart to stop."

"And why were you supposed to have done that too?"

"They cooked up some story about the will. I don't understand it. Anyway, the sheriff is telling me they had a will from Morgan claiming he didn't want any autopsy and wanted to be cremated right away. It turned over the operation to Savage. The funny part was they say he signed it that night—and no way did that happen—I was with him all night."

"So it's your word against the army of the Lord. Who were those bozos who knocked us out?"

"His doctor, his lawyer, and Savage."

"Neat," I said. "Somehow Savage won them over."

"Somehow is money. There's lots of it there."

"But didn't they have any loyalty to Morgan? Didn't he hire them?"

"Sure he did, and they were loyal as long as Morgan was with it. When he started to slip, they started looking out for themselves—they teamed up with the winner."

"Stacking the cards to make sure Savage won."

She nodded. "Poor Neeley," she said. "I really think Morgan leaned toward him. They went way back."

"Did he have the fire in his belly Savage does?"

"I doubt it. Certainly not enough to murder for it."

"You know, Dawn—take some good, heartfelt advice."

"What?"

"Let your dad help. He can afford the best attorney for you. It could make the difference between you getting out of here soon and swinging for a murder you didn't commit. These enemies are powerful. Alone you are so vulnerable."

She looked at me as though I'd lost my senses. "I'll take my chances," she said.

32

"Yaytz! She has rejected my help"—it was booming Bohem. "Talk sense to her."

I'd called to thank him for putting a nice sum in my bank account. Not the whole amount agreed upon, naturally, but a token of good faith, was I believe the way he put it.

I thought of Bohem as more token than faith.

Since the newspapers blabbed where Dawn was being held, I expected him to zoom up and take the matter personally in hand. I had misjudged Lajos. That was not his style. He considered himself too important a man to spend his time that way, he would send an emissary instead. No doubt a lawyer—perhaps the one Dawn had rejected on the phone.

The time seemed ripe for plucking. Advantage: mine. "Lajos," I said as though I were speaking jovially to an old friend—"is anything occurring to you?"

"What?" he asked, indicating a negative—"What is occurring?"

"Anyone you know uniquely positioned to help you?"

"Well…you…but…"

"But you're saving money."

"No, I, Yaytz—understand—I am distraught—my loved ones are in jeopardy." He spoke the words as though he were pitching a movie scenario. I don't think I ever met a man I could feel less sympathy for. Then why was I working for him? As I admitted in the beginning—money. And now that I'd gotten some of it, being imbued with human nature and all, I wanted more of it. I'd also become so involved in the Techsci scam I wanted to get to the bottom of it. For as Fannie Farmer said so often: "Bottoms are tops."

"So what is it worth to you to relieve that nagging distraught feeling you speak of?"

"Worth? I can't put a money sign on it. What do you want? I haf already made you generous proposal. Bring me my daughter, you weel be a rich man."

Not as rich as making movies that assault the senses from beginning to end I thought, but Bohem had the knack for aggravating himself and anything I could add would be redundant.

"Rich," I said at last, "is relative."

"Yeah?" he said. "You haf a rich relative?"

By marriage, I thought, but I didn't want to muddy the Pepsi Cola. "No," I said. "I would never be rich relative to you."

"You are splitting hairs," he said. "What do you say I add another tousand, you get Dawn out of jail?"

"Wow!" I said. "A whole thou! Most generous, Lajos. Must take you what to earn that? Five minutes?"

"I do not know…"

"No, no, I'm sure it's less."

"Much less."

"Two minutes, perhaps."

"No—less money in five minutes."

"I was thinking more on the order of one hundred thousand."

"On top of what you are already getting? That's preposterous." The way he said that indicated preposterous was one of the first words he'd learned in this country. Henceforth I would consider him a preposterous presence. I didn't really understand why he balked at my price. He wasn't going to pay me anyway. Perhaps it was his nature.

"Fifty tousand should be plenty," he weakened.

"You couldn't get a lawyer for that."

"Oh, yes I could—"

"To do what? Not try her case. You need proof before she goes to court or you're probably looking at closer to a million—those lawyers have noses for who can pay."

"Yaytz, you are being unreasonable again. I haf come up forty-nine tousand—you can come down tah same."

"Okay," I said, "forget it. Hire a lawyer she'll talk to, or take the rap publicly for not lending a helping hand to your daughter in her time of peril."

"Seventy-five!" he said.

"One hundred—"

"Yaytz! I weel meet you haf way—eighty-seven-five—"

"Not negotiable—"

"Yaytz!"

"Besides, if you got me on the cheap you wouldn't appreciate my work—and on top of that, I would resent your relentless chiseling so much I couldn't function at my best, which will certainly be required to spring Dawn."

"A good movie title, Spring Dawn." he said, so self-satisfied. " So weel you compromise?"

"I'll compromise."

"Good!"

"Ten thousand a day, and expenses."

"*Yaytz!*"

We haggled some more, but I thought it was all academic. "If you aren't going to pay, why not agree to a million?"

He finally caved.

"Have escrow draw the amendment," I said. "I'll call at five to see if they have your signed instructions. If they do, I'll go to work."

"How am I going to get it done so fast?"

"Messengers," I said, and hung up to add a touch of macho to the deal.

Giving my options about two minutes of thought, I headed back to the sheriff's office—the town of Solvang coming into cutesy view like they used to make Hollywood movies about. Fantasy Denmark no longer, as they say, cut it.

I put it down to occasional good fortune, which is bound to come your way if you live long enough, that I encountered a new delightful young woman in the head man's chair at the sheriff's station. There had been some ruckus lately about women being held back in the local law enforcement agencies, and I must say it didn't surprise me. Perhaps I'm provincial and old fashioned, but I don't see the fairest of all creatures in the history of the world pouncing on some PCP-laced muscle-bound six-foot six-inch, 250-pound escaped felon and overcoming him with her brute strength—or her charm for that matter. The girls' argument, I suppose, is that those who get the promotions are not the ones using brute force on the streets.

Sergeant Ula Quigley had other show-stopping attributes. She could have frozen any red-blooded American or un-American boy in his tracks, just by looking at him. She looked at me as I entered her (temporary) office, and she froze me in *my* tracks. There had to be some mistake—sheriffs were not supposed to be beautiful.

I don't know why I pictured her made-up with a low-cut cocktail dress instead of the severe sheriff's uniform and a face with only the color the maker put there. If that wasn't enough, she smiled at me, which would have put a lot of stronger men than me out of commission for days.

There were opening pleasantries which I didn't grace with space in my memory bank, and the next thing I remember is sitting across the desk from Sergeant Quigley telling her Dawn Bohem didn't kill J. Kent Morgan.

The Sergeant smiled. "I'm sure Miss Bohem will be glad to hear that. Do you have a substitute suspect?"

"Of course—"

"Isn't *you*, is it?"

"Oh no," I said. "Like Dawn, I had no reason to kill him."

"Who did?" she asked, and I was sure she had to know—was just testing me.

"The people who benefited from his death."

She looked at me with a cocked eye.

"Savage," I said. "The lawyer—the doctor—all

the troops that are taking over. You do know about Techsci and J. Kent Morgan, don't you?"

"Oh, yes," she said. "Kooks—pop psychology in the guise of religion. Morgan was hiding from every government agency you can name. The unholy ghost, we called him around here. Now you see him, now you don't."

"You didn't ever want to raid the place?"

"Some did, some didn't. He had his supporters as well as detractors in the department. When push came to shove, the consensus was he was getting old and ineffectual and what was going to follow him was bound to be worse—so we didn't rock the boat."

"With Dawn in jail, that's the party cant. You must know that."

She looked across her desk at my face—then nodded as though she saw the truth of my innocence there. She asked me in matching innocence—"Have you seen the will?"

"No, I..."

She pulled open a side drawer of the desk, pulled up a folder, opened it and handed it to me. A quick scan of the document took the wind out of my sailboats. Dawn had been made a beneficiary to the estate. Big bucks were due to her.

"Has Dawn seen this?"

She looked at me with a wry grin. "Now, that wouldn't be prudent, would it?"

"But you're risking me telling her?"

"How would you get to see her?"

I looked at Sergeant Quigley with new admiration. "Touché," I said.

"Unless we put you in a cell next to her—"

"Me?"

"Why not?" She was definitely playing with me.

"Look," I said, "Dawn was Morgan's best friend out there—the only one he trusted."

"Apparently," she said, pointing to the document.

"Oh, yes, this—it's not legit, you know. Did you find any prior wills? Wait, don't tell me—obviously you didn't. Did you see the signature on this? It's a scrawl—nothing like Morgan's signature."

"Two witnesses there—"

"Yeah. Did you question them?"

"Can't find them. Nobody knows…"

"Naturally. Tell you anything?"

"We have to assume the document is legit—until someone can prove otherwise—can you?"

"Dawn can. She was with him all day and night before he died. Nobody made him sign a new will. Jeez, isn't it just a little convenient?"

"Perhaps," she said, tenting her fingers in front of her flawless lips. "But she's a beneficiary. Will she maintain her story when she hears that?"

"Absolutely. Dawn was not in this for the money. Her father is filthy rich. I mean he's both. She left him—she is not a person motivated by money. Isn't it obvious they stuck this in to implicate her? If the state convicts her it will be moot anyway, and she'll never get the money. If the will is somehow authenticated, she will not be able to benefit from her crime. This will is a phony, believe me."

The sergeant sat with a maddening equipoise. I don't know what I expected—that she would throw off her uniform and dance on the desk? That might have been nice, but I don't think it was in the poker chips. At any rate, she just sat there regarding me over the tops of her tented fingers.

"All right, Mr. Yates," she said, "what do you suggest?"

She put me on the spot all right, but I was prepared. I had an answer, but I had no idea she'd go along with it.

33

"The boys will never go for it," she said, and I thought that was going to be the end of it. But she regarded me in that wary way all women in authority had of walking the line between safe and successful. "So it's going to have to be our secret."

I had a rush of relief—"Of course…"

"If it works, we'll be heroes. If it doesn't, I never heard of you."

Sergeant Quigley outfitted me from the undercover disguise locker. My hair and eyelashes, blondish in the original, were dyed black. I was given a deputy's uniform which fit more or less and fitted with a full beard and moustache that fooled even me.

The sun was past its zenith when we crawled into the official sheriff car. I looked at it with a question—Sergeant Quigley said, "We aren't in a position to take chances with an unmarked car. That bunch out there would just as soon shoot us for an invading army as look at us."

The air conditioning went on full blast in the

car. I didn't ask the Sergeant how she rated that. Rank hath its perks, I suspect.

As we left the last vestiges of civilization, I was again struck by what a beautiful woman Sergeant Quigley was. It was some miles before I said what was on my mind. The moonscape was coming into view, and I thought at any moment we would fall off the end of the lunar landscape.

"Sergeant," I began modestly, "perhaps it is a shortcoming of mine, but I don't associate law enforcement personnel with women who, ah, look as good as, ah, you. Does it—I mean, do you have any trouble being taken seriously because of it?"

She smiled, "Thank you, kind sir," she said. "Any woman has trouble being taken seriously in law enforcement—perhaps in *any* profession. Would it be easier if I were fat and ugly? I don't know, and I don't have the heart to put it to the test."

"Please don't," I said.

"How about you?" she asked. "I could say the same—you aren't the usual swaggering, macho private eye. Do *you* have trouble being taken seriously?"

"Touché!" I said. "In some venues, yes," I said, thinking of the ubiquitous Wemples, *pere et fille*—"in some cases it's an asset—to be a nonthreatening questioner."

"What about with your clients? Don't you have trouble getting cases?"

"Oh, no—I have as many as I want. To understand it, one has only to understand the heart of man. I work contingency. I don't solve their problem, I don't get a dime."

"Really? You pay expenses too?"

I nodded. "You bet. Of course, since I gamble, my fees are high, and I usually work for the very rich—and if you know anything about the very rich, they like to hang on to their money. A thousand a day and expenses scares the liver out of them. They know they could run up a significant bill and have nothing to show for it, whereas a hundred grand if I find the kid—more if I solve the murder that will release hundreds of millions from a will, put into that perspective it sounds reasonable to them. Besides, I don't doubt my meekness of demeanor goes a long way toward their deciding to trust me. The super-rich can always grind you to fertilizer if they don't like what you're doing."

As we trundled through the desolate landscape, I asked, "How did this mysterious death pass the coroner?"

"Not as difficult as it seems. He—purportedly—signed a statement saying he didn't want an autopsy. A medical doctor signs a death certificate and, unless we have some evidence of foul play, we accept it. Poof"—she snapped her fingers—"next thing you know he's in flames."

"You mean a *doctor* could *fake* a death certificate?" I was being purposely naïve.

"Now, Gil," she said with a feminine purr that threatened to put me off my feed, "in this business we learn that an exalted profession is no guarantee of an exalted person."

There was a major hub-bub when we showed up at the Techsci gate. The guards were obviously flustered—they had guns and probably instructions to use them if necessary—but on two uniformed sheriffs? Probably not good PR.

There were a flurry of telephone calls and inquiries of us about the nature of our visit. Sergeant Quigley was polite but firm, and with each protracted stall of her request she grew more terse—finally she said—"You know, sir, we are here to investigate a murder. Do you want to open the gate or shall I drive through it?"

He opened the gate and gave her instructions to the new mansion, which meant we turned left at the top of the T.

Savage was there to greet us when we parked with all the warmth he could muster, which was not to say he was going to melt any igloos with it.

"How may I help you?" he asked.

"We'd like to ask a few questions," the sergeant said. "May we come in?"

"Certainly," he said, far from certain.

From cursory and surreptitious glances it appeared Savage had moved into the mansion; lock, stock and corncob. He was using the commodious library at the end of the hall as an office.

It seemed evident he was not the sort to use it for books. The walls of shelves were virtually empty. He saw us surveying the acres of empty book shelves. "Oh, the shelves. We'll get some of Morgan's books in them eventually. He wrote a lot of books, and liked to be surrounded by them." He tossed off a mini shrug—not the kind that would burn any calories. "Personally, I don't have that need."

A weak smile came to Ula Quigley's lips—as if

from nowhere. "It was good of you to see us," she said. I loved the line. As though he had a choice! "I'm Sergeant Quigley, and this is Deputy Parker."

He nodded his head with the same underexertion he'd used with the shrug. He barely looked at me. The disguise was holding, though I had visions of the beard falling off and me being "made" as they say.

The sergeant got down to business: "I understand there was a man named Bill Yates out here. A private investigator. Do you know what happened to him?"

"I don't know anyone by that name."

"Perhaps I have it wrong, Gil Bates?"

"No."

"Any private investigators visit here recently?"

"Well, if there was, he's gone."

"Where?"

"I don't know."

"He seems to have disappeared."

"Not my doing...if he has."

She fixed him with a pretty good gaze.

"What about Suzanne Bohem, Dawn's mother?"

"I think she left when they arrested Dawn."

"You think?"

"I don't keep tabs on the comings and goings of every person here."

"No? That's not what I heard."

"You heard wrong then." He was stonewalling with the best of them.

"So she has *disappeared* also?" Her emphasis was incredulous.

He shrugged.

"Perhaps walked out with Gil Yates? That is it—
Gil Yates—mean anything now?"

His eyes got funny.

"Let me help you." Sergeant Quigley said, "Our
prisoner, Dawn Bohem, tells us he was with her the
night Morgan died…the night you came into his trailer
with the doctor and lawyer and gave her a knockout
shot."

"Well, I told you before—Dawn Bohem has
trouble with the truth."

"Ever have trouble with the truth yourself, Mr.
Savage?"

He just glared at her.

"Mind if we look around?"

He turned on the old ice machine—"Techsci is
sacred church property," he said. "But if you have a
search warrant, go ahead."

It was a good bluff. We didn't have one.

"All right, if you feel that way, we'll get one. I
just thought if this was a real religion, there would be
some charity toward your fellow creatures, but perhaps
not. I must confess I always get this suspicion whenever
anyone rejects a request to look around—that something is amiss."

"Ever hear of the right of privacy?" he asked.

"Privacy? Suzanne Bohem's privacy? If she wants
it, she can easily have it. Something doesn't seem right,
Mr. Savage—the mother of a girl doped and accused of
murder and dragged out of here unconscious, doesn't
care enough to visit her daughter? So Suzanne either
disappeared like this Yates person or is still here. We'd
just like to look for her. Would you object to that? We

aren't talking about going through anybody's drawers."

He tightened his lips. I suppose if I had to use one word to explain Savage's character it would be "tight."

"Get your search warrant, Deputy, then we'll talk. Then you can have your drawers and anything else you want."

"You'll give us Suzanne?"

"If she's here and wants to go with you—certainly."

In spite of his words, Savage gave us the impression if we wanted to come back we'd have to shoot our way in.

And Sergeant Ula Quigley gave him the impression if that was what it took, that's what we would do.

34

On our way out of the Techsci compound we were graced with a Techsci escort. Savage tried to make it seem a perk for important people, but we knew better.

I told Quigley about my incarceration in their lovely prison and pointed to it as we passed it. The Sergeant slammed on the brakes, the guardians behind us were not happy.

We got out of the car.

"Where are you going?" the driver of the escort car asked us with some astonishment.

"Like to take a look at your facilities," she said, "if you don't mind."

"I mind," he said. It was old Phil Culp from my safari to L.A., and he didn't recognize me either. People just don't seem to look at people—fortunately.

"Oh?" she said, as though his denial was down right freakish. "Why not? This is a *church*, isn't it?"

"It is," he said firmly.

"So what's in this building?" she asked, nodding toward the multipurpose structure where I had sat in my chains—and where, at another end, the chosen ate their meals.

"Cafeteria—offices—"

"And you don't want me to see that?"

"I have my orders," he said. "I understand you're coming back with a search warrant. You can see it then."

"Same as it is now?"

He nodded with his lips tightly pursed.

"So wouldn't it be a lot simpler to let me see it now? Save precious gasoline for this precious planet your late leader was always going on about."

He shook his head once. "Orders," he repeated, as though it was the only word in his vocabulary.

"Orders," she repeated.

He snapped off a nod.

"What's your name?" she asked.

"Phil Culp."

She took a notebook from her back pocket, and with deliberation wrote his name in it.

"Hey," he said, "what are you doing?"

"Orders," she said.

"Orders?" He didn't like the sound of that.

"I have orders to cite anyone who interferes with our investigation."

"Hey—I'm not interfering. You need a search warrant, and you don't have one."

"Um hmm," she said.

"And I only work here, I don't give any orders."

"Except to us."

"Well…"

"That's all right Mr. Culp," she said. "Remember all those Nazis were only following orders too." And while his mouth was agape his brain searching for the perfect response, she got back behind the wheel of our sheriff's car. She put it in gear and we drove off toward the gate. "You gave up too easily," I said.

She smiled. "Not accidentally," she said. "My hunch is Suzanne is in that prison. Now they're on the spot and they can't leave her there."

"So when we get back, she'll be gone."

"I don't think that's the way it will play out."

"Oh? How will it?"

We got through both gates without further interruptions—Techsci Phil Culp saw us out of the main gate and watched us drive off the moonscape.

"My inkling is they can't let her out inside. Too much risk—what mother, given her daughter is in jail, falsely accused of murder, is going to sit still while her fellow psychology nuts frame her daughter for a crime she knows she didn't commit? So, I say they are going to give her the same treatment they gave you."

"The fields?"

"Abandon her, doped up, in the open country. And my take on that is Suzanne will not survive as you did. She's smaller—frailer, the drug will last longer in her body—they may even give her enough to kill her— if they've found something that can't be traced in a blood test or autopsy."

"There is such a thing?"

"Oh yes—and more deadly and elusive are the things that kill you in combination—neither by itself being lethal. Or something that does its work, and by the time the body is found, it has disappeared from the system."

"So what can we do? By the time we get the warrant, she'll be gone."

"That's why we're going to park and wait for them to come out. I don't think it's going to be long. Fortunately it's getting dark and we'll be harder to see. Now let's look for some terrain that gives us a modicum of cover."

"What if they take her out back?"

She shook her head. "I don't think they can risk leaving her on their property. They didn't do that to you—"

"How do you know?"

"Where you were picked up—more miles from here than you could walk. And as far as we know, they think you died there and gave the vultures a happy lunch. Can they get out another way?"

"Not that I know. No roads, anyway."

"Well, we'll take our chances."

We found something of a hill, perhaps a mile or two from the gate. It was pretty much dark now—with clouds covering the sliver of moon that presented itself to the earth at this juncture.

She cut the engine, sighed, and looked over the front seat at me and smiled. "Geez, how long it's been since I parked with a fella on a deserted road. You know, you really look good in uniform—ever think of signing up?"

I didn't have the answer right away, but I didn't give up. When it came to me I was glad for my patience. "If I could be guaranteed a boss as beautiful as you—you can start calling me deputy."

She smiled a soft, womanly smile, not a tough sheriff-grin. "You're sweet." She cut the engine, sighed, and looked across the front seat at me smiling.

Suddenly, the expected car flew by, travelling at an aggressive clip.

Ula started the engine, threw the car into gear and eased out onto the road without turning on the lights. We could see the rear lights of the car ahead.

"Keep your eyes on those lights," she said, "We don't want to lose them."

"Think they know we're here?" I asked.

"I don't think so," she said. "A deserted road like this—at night—you only become aware of cars by their lights."

"This is not going to be so easy if we get out on a busy road," I said. "But I guess we'll cross that river when we come to the bridge."

She smiled. "Not a bad idea," she said.

"Where was I picked up?" I asked.

"A ways from here," she said.

"Think they'll go to the same spot?"

"Doubt it. Unless they want to see if you're still there. Of course we don't even know if they have Suzanne in the car."

"Good bet, though," I said.

"Good bet."

"Why don't you call the helicopter?" I asked.

"One reason," she said, "and he's sitting next to me. This is not what we call a routine chase—I've no doubt if I were caught at this it would be the end of my career."

"But you're only trying to get the bad guys—"

"Oh yeah, but I got too far outside the box taking you with me in that getup. As it is, private dicks are not the pride and joy of those of us who work as grunts in uniform."

When we got to the main highway, we were obliged to turn on our lights. Apparently they saw us because they accelerated at a break-back speed.

Up ahead, the car passed a trailer truck and when we went to pass, another car came toward us so we were obliged to hang back. Then the truck put on its brakes suddenly. Ula found it prudent to brake—the truck rolled to a stop—by the time it did, we noticed the body by the side of the road.

I didn't even have to look—I knew it was Suzanne.

35

Sergeant Ula Quigley pulled off the road just past the body and jumped out. I followed.

She bent over Suzanne and said—"Suzanne's alive—give me a hand—put her in the back."

The truck driver was with us, materializing from nowhere—"Give you a hand?" he said—"Call 911?"

"Open the back door," the Sergeant said. "We'll get her to a hospital." We lifted Suzanne—she was like a hammock between us.

"You see it happen?" the Sergeant asked.

"Yeah," he said. "They slowed, pulled over, dumped her and sped on."

"See them?"

"Not well. Two men."

"Description?"

"Not that easy to tell—one older, one younger. Younger one doing the heavy work—pushing her out. Got the license—one of those Ford SUVs," he said.

We got Suzanne in the back seat, the truck driver gave Sergeant Quigley the license number, his name, Nuncio something, and phone number.

In the car, Ula radioed headquarters to look for the SUV and intercept it before it got back into the Techsci compound. "I'm taking the victim to Cottage Hospital—she's unconscious and has some bruises. Over and out."

She turned off the radio and turned on the flashers, made a U-turn and headed to fabled Santa Ynez.

"Also against regulations," she muttered.

"What is?"

"I should have kept up the pursuit—radioed location of the body—sent an ambulance."

"Why?"

"Why? Because law enforcement is my game. I'm not a doctor. I should have radioed for an ambulance and pursued the bad guys," she said, then added, "Besides, I'm off duty now and I'm driving an official car."

"Will it get you into trouble?" I asked.

"Probably. Listen, I'm going to have to drop you off at your hotel. Get the uniform off as soon as you can and hide it. Lay low. I'll be in touch."

"You don't want me to go to the hospital with you?"

"Can't risk it," she said. "Around the corner to the station."

She pulled up in front of my hotel—I stuck out my hand to bid her goodbye.

She looked at it and smiled. "Okay, trooper," she said, and shook it—holding perhaps a smidgen longer than regulations would have it.

I watched her go, then ducked into the hotel and made it up to my room without seeing a soul. I looked in the mirror and got quite a kick out of what I saw. I was no longer surprised no one had recognized me—I didn't recognize myself.

I took off the beard and uniform, but left the hair color. I thought I looked rather dashing with the dark eyebrows—Latin-lover type.

The quiet time I devoted to my Bohem strategy. How to wrap up the case and earn my fee with one of the subjects half dead in the hospital and the other in jail...not to mention my client looking for every nuance and loophole to stiff me.

Exhaustion seeped through my bones, so I lay those weary bones on the bed for a few moments rest before I'd think about going down for dinner.

The phone woke me.

"Still awake?" Ula asked.

"I am now."

"Oh, sorry—I just thought you'd want a report. Suzanne is alive, but barely. The doctors won't commit. Apparently she got the same elixir they gave Dawn and you—but something went wrong. I'll keep you posted—I'll stop by in the morning to pick up the...costume."

"Yeah," I said, sleep subduing my voice. "Happy Halloween."

"The same to you," she said, and hung up.

It was not easy to get back to sleep. I ruminated over the options with Lajos Bohem. How brokenhearted would he be if Suzanne died? It would give him a plausible excuse for not having his wife by his side in sickness and health, for rich or for poor, if death did them part. Should I rush to tell him her condition or not? A conundrum. Of one thing I was convinced: I was happy I would not have to look for the killer—not that there was much mystery about it, but they had seen to it the evidence was scant to nonexistent.

I decided to do a little finagling with Lajos Bohem, Schlockmeister, in regard to his accused and jailed daughter. Would there be any harm in telling him I was instrumental in her release? A flexible word, instrumental. But it wasn't a case of where I'd be gladdened in my heart to see father and daughter reconciled. Oh, I could play a few fanfares to family values, and the rewards for sticking together through thick and not so thick, but I'm afraid in Lajos' case the tune would go flat. Dawn was an adult and no longer required to be an appendage to his ego.

I dozed off again, this time for the night. The phone woke me again.

"Up and at 'em," the Sergeant said.

"Aye, aye, sir—or madam as the case may be."

"Suzanne had a rough night, but they think she may be coming out of it. I'm swinging by to pick up the Halloween—want some breakfast?"

"Not a bad idea—since I foreswore dinner for the cause."

"I'm looking into a citation for you—be there in ten minutes or so. Oh, and they got the guys who dumped Suzanne. They're questioning them now."

I was ready—downstairs—with a brown bag package under my arm. Well, all right, I was out on the quaint old sidewalks, pacing.

I didn't recognize her at first—she drove a small purple thing instead of an official car—she laughed when she saw me hoofing the sidewalks.

"Well, deputy," she said when she pulled next to me and rolled down her window, "watcha got in the package there?"

I dropped it on her lap. "A hot potato," I said. "I had these paranoid visions of your cohorts picking me up—and me withstanding the hose torture about where I got the uniform—not breathing your name until my dying breath—"

"At which time you thought, the devil with it, and blurted it out—" she was amused. "Any reason we shouldn't eat in the hotel?" she asked.

"Not as long as the uniform is in your possession." There I noticed she wore a dress—a gingham thing that mode her look down-home. "Hey, where's the sheriff suit?"

"Saving it for Halloween."

"Hey, don't tell me—you aren't really a sheriff— you're an impersonator yourself."

"Right," she said.

"Well, you've got to admit, you look more like a girl headed for a hoedown than a sheriff."

"You talking about the pot bellied guys, or John Wayne?"

"Am I wrong?"

"I hope not. Have you checked out?"

"No."

"Good—we can put it on your expense account." Then she laughed. I guess she remembered I had no expense account. And if I had one with Lajos Bohem, he'd find a way out of paying it.

She parked and we went into an almost empty dining room and sat at a rear table. A corn fed waitress brought menus and returned in a jiffy to take the order.

I had oatmeal garnished like one of those curry chickens—Ula did something with fruit and pancakes.

I endeavored to enlist her in my scheme. She listened politely, all the while I awaited for her kibosh.

"I suppose you'd like to get Dawn out of jail," I said.

"Doesn't seem much reason to hold her now," she agreed.

"Her own protection?" I offered, hopeful.

"Oh, I expect she'd be safe—if you took her back to her father in Hollywood, USA."

I brightened, and it must have been noticeable because she smiled broadly as though we were both in on the same secret. "Well, yes...good...but...how about if we don't rush it—giving me some time...and leverage with the old man."

"How long would that be?"

"Depends how recalcitrant he is. Couple days to a week."

"A *week!* That might be a little tough. Well...we're going to need her to prosecute—"

"How are you going to do that?"

"The big question—not a lot to go on—not much DNA in an unholy ghost."

I diddled with my oatmeal. "Yeah."

"The three I's are your friend—" she said.

"Three I's?"

"Inertia, Insouciance and Indolence. Leave it to the boys. Till they figure it out, you should have plenty of time."

"I don't know. It usually takes longer than you think, but with the mighty mogul, Lajos Bohem, you never know. He is a man, I've decided, devoted to appearance, and that could be our salvation. At any rate, whatever you can do will be appreciated." I wanted to be the hero of this piece. I wanted some leverage to earn my fee.

"Roger—"

"I'm Gil—"

She laughed. "We can always say we are keeping her for her own protection. Especially while her mother is still in danger."

"Twenty-four hours," Ula said when she parted from me. "I can't guarantee we can hold Ms. Bohem longer. She really should be visiting her mother."

36

It didn't come to me quickly, but after Sergeant Ula Quigley left I finally got an idea. Given the time constraint, I didn't see another solution, let alone a better one.

I called the studio office of Lajos Bohem. He came right on the phone. "What do you haf, Yaytz—good news, I hope?"

I couldn't help speculating about why he was so keen on wanting his women back. I couldn't imagine him paying much attention to them while he had them. Was it the old story—we only want what we can't have? His ego was bruised at their desertion. He probably envisioned a triumphal return with chariots and banner, drums and bugles—down the main drag of the studio with stars blowing him kisses and decking him out in garlands of orchids. I could see him, all obsequious smiles, with a huge horseshoe of red roses weighting him down as though he had just won the Kentucky Derby. And I had no trouble envisioning him as part of a horse.

"Good news and bad news," I said. "Isn't that

how it always goes?"

"Good news first."

Not so fast, I thought. I'm going to mete this out to my advantage. "Your wife is in the hospital."

"Tat's tah good news? She always was a hypochondriac."

"This time it's real."

"Real? What is it? What did she do?"

"Wrong place at the wrong time. Someone had to get her out of the way. They almost killed her."

"Savages!"

Like your movies, I thought.

"Haf you got Dawn out of jail?"

"Imminent," I said, but it was not a word he brought over from Hungary.

"What?"

"I'm working on it—any day now."

There was a disappointed silence from his direction.

"Lajos?" I said.

"Hmm?"

"You've got to come up here."

"What? Impossible. I'm in tah middle of tah most important picture I haf ever made."

Now that stopped me very low temperature-wise. My first thought was I didn't know people still made Z pictures, but I kept it to myself. "What is Citizen Kane next to your loved ones?" I asked, and I could tell he was pleased.

"My loved ones, ya," he said. "Tat is why I am paying you."

"That's news to me," I said. "The paying part."

"You know better, Yaytz!" he almost shouted. "I

haf paid you once and tere is more waiting. If you deliver tah goods," he added, duly commodifying his quoted loved ones.

"All right, bring the check when you come."

"Come—I told you—"

"Oh, yes, the most important movie in history."

"Don't mock me, Yaytz. You want to complete tah job, or you want me to get someone else?"

"That's a good one, Lajos," I said—not as good as his most important movie, perhaps, but good nonetheless. "You know your wife and daughter won't talk to anyone else if they think they are associated with you."

"You poison tem—" he said, "why would tey talk to *you*?"

"My innate charm?"

I think I heard him grunt.

"All right—you want them back?"

"Ya."

"Here's what it'll take—one, the certified check drawn on the escrow funds. Two, your presence at the escrow company with your signed and notarized authorization to release the certified check to me on my delivering your aforementioned loved ones, and you laying eyes on them."

"Unacceptable."

"Why?"

"It is jest as before. You whisk tem before my eyes and you already want tah money."

"That's what the agreement says."

"I want time with tem. I must haf time."

"How much time?"

"At least a week."

"They'll never go for it. If you had told me that in the beginning I wouldn't have taken the job."

"You'd turn down two hundred tousand dollars—I don't believe it."

"Believe it," I said. "I take tough cases, but not impossible ones."

"Yaytz—Yaytz—tere must be a solution."

"You know their fear is you will trick them. If I leave them alone with you, you'll kidnap and incarcerate them in some unpleasant way. They're afraid you'll try to deprogram them."

"Why would tey fear tat? If teir beliefs are strong, tey will hold onto tem."

"So you were planning deprogramming?"

"Well…it is an option."

"Let me tell you something. It may not be necessary. They killed Morgan, and blamed it on Dawn—they drugged Suzanne and tried to leave her for dead—not the kind of thing that encourages loyalty."

I could hear him thinking through the silence. And I wondered—how would the mogul react if his wife and daughter showed up on his doorstep and said, "We're back." I think he'd be aghast. I don't think he wanted anything to do with either one of them, but his vanity was wounded—with first one leaving him, then the other, and being a control-freak, he couldn't stand the appearance of impotence he imagined their actions caused.

"Well," he said at last, "give me time to tink—it may be unnecessary, as you say."

I caught his gist—too fast. He was twisting my words to his interest. If Dawn and Suzanne were free of Techsci, my services were no longer required. He knew where they were—he could take over from there—and the unspoken obvious: not pay my fee. I visualized a protracted legal battle, motions, pleas, depositions, interrogatories—he'd spend 10 million to keep me from $200,000. Well, I'd already gotten fifty—better then a kick in the pantaloons as they say—so why didn't I give up? Right is right after all—but of course, right isn't everything. Sometimes it isn't *anything*. Perhaps it was a character flaw that I would outgrow someday, but I honored my agreements, I expected others to do the same.

"Sorry," I said, going to tough-guy. "Time we don't have. When they release Dawn and Suzanne, you are the last person they will want to see."

"Maybe," he said, unconvinced.

"I am your only hope. Honor your contract, and you can make your pitch to both of them."

"I weel call you—what's your number?"

"I'll call you," I said—"tomorrow—nine in the morning—" I hung up. I always felt a little icky after talking to him.

37

Call it an epiphany, call it a revelation; I don't know what to credit it to, but that night as I lay in bed trying to put Lajos Bohem out of my mind, it came to me. I was handling it all wrong. I was bogged down in principle—I was right, darn it, and I was going to cram it down his throat, if I lost the deal doing so. Only he wasn't biting, and his throat was closed to the public.

At nine the next morning, as promised, I called Mogul Bohem. Before I could get a word in, he started his cannons: "I haf been thinking, Yaytz—and since tah situation has changed, I tink your fee is too high."

I didn't say anything. After a few seconds it rankled. "Yaytz? Are you there?"

"Yes."

"Did you hear me?"

"I heard you."

"Well—what do you say?"

"You're right," I said.

"What was tat?"

"I said you were right."

"I am right?"

"Um hmmm."

Silence. Finally—"You mean you agree wit me?"

"Yes."

"So we can renegotiate?"

"Not necessary," I said. "You set the fee. I'm sure you'll be fair."

"Of course," he said, and I could see him stick out a proud chest. "Let's see—it was two hundred, wasn't it?"

"Yes."

"And you already extorted fifty out of me, correct?"

"The amount is correct. I don't know if I want to agree with the extortion part."

"So what do you say to anoter five or ten tousand?"

"If that's what you think is fair, fine."

"Fine?" It was obvious Mr. Bohem couldn't believe his eardrums. I really expected he would ask for some of the fifty back—half or more, so I was making progress. "All right, I will redo tah contract."

"Oh, don't bother. I trust you—"

"You *trust* me?"

"Yes."

"And none of tat escrow business? You can bring tem here—to my office?"

"If that's what you want."

"Good! I weel haf a party—a homecoming."

"That would be very nice," I said.

"Good!"

"I'll talk to your women—we'll be in touch."

"When?"

"I hope later today."

"Tat is good work, Meester Yaytz. Good work."

I hung up thinking I was taking ice cream from a baby, and the baby didn't have a clue about my idea for fleecing him out of the whole 150 grand.

I picked the phone right up and called L.A. information for the Dungeon on Melrose.

I called the number and got an answering machine with a message that they opened at three PM. "If your pants are on fire and you just *have* to leave a message for someone, wait for the beep."

Beep. "This is Gil Yates for Sophie Weintraub. I interviewed her a while ago about her friend—who is now in jail and in urgent need of her support. I can be reached at the Grand Hotel in Los Olivos—" and I left the number. "Leave a message and I'll call back with particulars. Urgent!"

Then I went over to the Solvang sheriff's station. Luckily Sergeant Ula Quigley was on duty so I got right in to Dawn.

She was in moderate spirits—I think she knew she was getting out—but before I got far into my spiel about her dad, she blurted, "I don't want anything to do with the creep."

"I know that," I said. "And if my plan works, you won't have to."

"And why would I agree to your plan?"

Of course it all came back to money. I offered her $25,000 for essentially one day's work. She tried not to let on, but she was interested.

I told her about the fee arguments her father and I had, going back to the beginning—as well as our most recent conversation. "So the twenty-five grand is contingent on my getting the one hundred fifty I'm due." I'd given up on the fifty thousand dollars for both of them staying with Lajos. It wasn't a realistic option.

"How am I going to do that?"

"I have some ideas," I told her. I laid out my plan—she was amused, but not noticeably adverse.

We concentrated on the first step—the initial phone call to her father. Together we wrote the script.

"Hi, Dad, it's Dawn. I'm doing okay, and you? Dad, I think it's time we bury the hatchet," (I said hammer, but Dawn corrected me), "in spite of our past differences. I'd like to forgive and forget and start over."

(Here we expected him to express delight and ask how soon she could come).

"Anytime you want."

(Good!)

"I have just one request."

(Anything).

"The reason I'm still alive and Mom is still alive is a man named Gil Yates...oh, you know him—yes, well, I understand you did, and he has mentioned in passing he was sacrificing his fee to reunite us—and Dad, well, I just wouldn't feel right about it. You have all the money in the world and he has so little. I know you think I am a bleeding heart liberal, but if anyone deserves to be handsomely rewarded it's Gil Yates. He risked his life—was left for dead—Mom *would* have been dead without him. Is that worth anything to you? I understand you offered him five thousand of his one hundred fifty. Tsk, tsk, tsk, saving money again. You know, Mom's in the hospital. She could use the support. I can't see her 'cause I'm locked up, but you could. How about coming up?"

(Oh, love to—far too busy—making the most important film of my career.)

It was a leverage play. Ask the impossible, the possible won't seem so difficult.

"Well, I'm ready to do my part—but understand, if they let me out of this jail that too will be Gil's doing. So here's my offer—you think it over, and if I'm worth it to you, I'll come." (Of *course* you're worth it, but I don't like blackmail. It's like ransom.)

"So you have a certified cashier's check made out to Gil Yates for one hundred fifty thousand—we'll come down there. Gil will come in—you give him the check, and I'm all yours—I'll be in your office just as soon as Gil signals he got payment. I trust—in this new era of trust—you won't try to kidnap me—because it could get very messy."

(What do you mean?)

"Just a fair warning. Oh, Daddy, I *want* this to work—I hope you do too. You think it over. Gil will be in touch."

And she did beautifully. Deserved an academy award. I knew we had him. All I had to do was deliver the goods.

When I got back to the hotel I was handed a message and phone number from Sophie Weintraub. I called. When I identified myself, she flew to the ceiling. "I'm *needed?* Tell me when and where and I'll be right there."

"Now," I said hopefully. "Can you come now?"

"Right this minute?"

"Yes. 101 North, to 154 to Los Olivos—I'll meet you at the Grand Hotel. It'll take you a couple of hours, so I'll be here from one to two. Drive carefully."

In another hour I called Lajos Bohem. In keeping with my new outlook I'd stopped referring to him as the mighty mogul and Uriah Heep.

When he answered, I could tell he was on the same ceiling as Sophie Weintraub. He began regaling me with his good fortune. "And I know," he said, "once Dawn is home, Suzanne weel follow on her own. She only went to bring Dawn back. So I am arranging a homecoming party—a few friends—a warm welcome."

"Dawn might like it more low key," I said. "Just the two of you at first—" I hoped he wouldn't take my suggestion, but past experience in Lajos' contrariness led me to believe we were on firm *terra*.

"Oh, plenty of time for tat. Tis is a big moment for me—the prodigal daughter returns. It must be celebrated. And, oh, Yaytz, I won't be quibbling about tah fee. Tere will be a check here for you when you arrive."

"That's awfully big of you," I said. "But you know, I'm leaving it up to you."

And butterflies give Pepsi Cola.

38

The arrangements were made.

Sophie Weintraub came to my hotel a little after one. She made good time.

"Want lunch?" I asked her.

"No—I want to get right to Dawn."

We drove over to the Sheriff's station in my rental. She'd done enough driving.

The reunion was perfect. No one could have written it better. Hugs, kisses, tears.

I supposed the relaxed atmosphere at the jail was indicative of Dawn's status. She was about to be released, but I didn't let on. I didn't want either Dawn or Sophie to get cocky. Keep the strings taut. They play better in tune.

When the ladies came back to earth, I brought up the homecoming party.

"I'm not going to that," Sophie Weintraub said.

"I'm not either," Dawn agreed.

"I don't blame you," I said. "But let's consider the opportunity."

"Why does he have to have a *party?* Can't we do something for once not for the public?"

"You might be the first person to change human nature," I said, "but if you are, I doubt it will start with Lajos Bohem."

"A-men," Sophie said.

"I suggest we look at the bright side, and make some plans."

From there on it was a creative masterpiece—a rip-roaringly successful session of *Can you top this?* It was amusing, creative and delightful. After each idea which was more clever than the last, Dawn would cry— "Cut! Print!" as the directors of her father's movies would. We all applauded.

Sergeant Ula Quigley gave us a syllabus for release and we got her out without an attorney. The official suspicion had shifted to Savage, the attorney and the doctor. Proof promised to be more elusive.

Our first stop was the Cottage Hospital, where we found Suzanne on the street to recovery.

Dawn told her our plan. She endorsed it with a happy clap of her hands, but demurred about participating.

A nurse came in and told us Suzanne should be ready for release in a couple of days. We agreed to keep that information to ourselves until Dawn made her appearance and I got my money. I had, after all, already produced Suzanne and fulfilled my contractual obligation on her.

I called Lajos Bohem from the hospital pay phone. He was thrilled at the news and asked to talk to Dawn, but I told him it was best not to interrupt—she wasn't that strong and we'd be in L.A. whenever he wanted us.

"I haf alerted everyone—so tah sooner tah better."

"Tomorrow?"

"I weel haf to hustle, but it weel be worth it."

Back in the room, I learned Suzanne had not decided what she would do. Going back to Techsci was not an option.

We said goodbye to Suzanne and headed to a downtown hotel where I got Dawn and Sophie a room. They could relax, be tourists, rejuvenate their lives while I returned to the Sheriff's station in Santa Ynez.

Sergeant Quigley took a break, and we walked around the block.

"It *was* fun," she said, as though I had argued the opposite (a la Gil Yates). "You ever come this way again, be sure and pop in to say hello."

"I'll be watching the case," I said. "What do you think your chances of nailing Savage, the doc and lawyer are?"

She frowned, then brightened. "We'll give it our best shot," she said. "Fifty-fifty would be optimistic."

"Well, maybe they'll roast in hell," I said.

She pursed her lips and shook her head. "They don't believe in it," she said. "With that kind of conclusion it's going to be tough going. It's the kind of case where you almost have to wait until one of them breaks.—one of them becomes disgruntled because he didn't get his share—something fluky."

"I'll be rooting for you."

"Thanks—" we'd made the trip around the

block. I gave her a hug outside the station house and watched her go inside. She was one good looking woman.

But she didn't look back.

The next morning Dawn, Suzanne and I drove in tandem to the Santa Barbara airport, where I turned in my rental car. Then the three of us proceeded south in Sophie's funked up 25 year-old Cadillac with, would you believe two fuzzy red dice hanging from the rearview mirror and faux zebra seat covers? I sat in the back.

An hour before we arrived we made our last minute plans. I would go in first, check it out, get the check. The women would change their clothes in the bathroom, then make their entrance.

The trip passed quickly as they caught up on old times in the front seat.

At one point I asked, "Dawn, what was your relationship with your father really like? Growing up, I mean."

"He wanted a boy to carry on the glorious name and oeuvre of Lajos Bohem. I had the feeling he would have settled for a dog—but not this," she said, pointing to her chest. "Dogs are more obedient—and that's the way he treated me: as a pet who displayed excitement at the great man coming home, with perhaps a pat behind the ears. Then it was on to more important matters…like adding to the body count in his flicks."

"No kidding," Sophie asked, "would you go back to living with him?"

Dawn didn't answer right away—then she giggled. "When we get through, I don't think that's going to be an option. Do you have room?"

"For you—anytime."

The man at the gate of the studio in Culver City was dressed in his rent-a-cop uniform. He had been primed to expect us, and he was all smiles as he directed us to the special parking space reserved for us. I could be mistaken, but I thought I noted a look of appreciation for Sophie's car in his eyes.

The ladies let me out at the entrance of the building just inside the gate where Lajos Bohem created his monstrosities.

Before I hit the door to his Mussolini office I heard the hubbub of a major party in process. When I got to the open door I saw the "few friends" Bohem had promised turned into a veritable army of sycophants, hangers-on, butt-kissers, flunkies, and indentured servants—and my, there were a lot of them.

When Lajos' eyes drifted to me, a frown came to his brow. In an age when people were super-sensitive about the smoke from cigarettes, Lajos seemed to flaunt his on the edge of his ciggy holder.

"Oh, it's you, Yaytz," he said with some relief in his voice, coming over to greet me as one of the aforementioned categories—I wouldn't venture to guess which one. "I didn't recognize you. It's tah hair, isn't it? You dyed it."

"In the line of duty," I said. "Helped save your wife's life," I said with very little effort at modesty.

"Yees, yees," he said, dismissing me. "I'll haf to hear about it sometime. In tah meantime, come and join tah party. We haf shrimps and stuffed mushrooms—crab legs, beef, turkey, ham—over here's some champagne—" he held up the glass he had in his hand, half full. Or was it half empty? One or the other.

"If you don't see what you want, just tell me, I weel get it for you—we even haf pastrami and pickles on rye," he gave me a knowing glance, which I speculated might be anti-Semitic.

I'll say this for the Hollywood crowd—they know how to throw parties that look expensive. I was hard pressed to think of anything I might want that wasn't on display.

The girls passing the hors d'oeuvres were dressed in long, severe skirts and neck-topped blouses. In spite of his ridiculous, prurient movies, word was Lajos Bohem was something of a prude.

Lajos made a sheepish confession to me: "I took tah liberty of inviting tah press," he said. "So many of tem came—tere has been so much talk of estrangement of my girls, tis reunion is news. And my peecture is coming out. The publicity weel not hurt—" he hurled me a knowing wink as though we were old pals.

"Photographers too?" I asked, looking around for the *paparazzi*.

"Well, yes, certainly. A picture is worth a tousand words." He was so pleased with himself—holding himself and his cigarette holder as though Noel Coward was choreographing his every move.

"You know," he said, "tis may be tah happiest day of my life—I know how tah father of tah prodigal son felt—you know, in the Bible," he added, in case I was illiterate.

While he talked, he kept stealing glances at the door—"My girl is coming, yes?"

"Oh, yes," I assured him. "Just parking the car and freshening up. It was a long drive."

He seemed satisfied. "You know," he said in an expansive mood, "I haf been a busy man—with my films—but I always had time for my loved ones. I was a veery good family man. You know how important it is to put your stamp on your kid."

I thought of my own kids: August, the wannabe ballet dancer whose "profession" drives his grandfather, Daddybucks, up the wall, and Felicity, the perpetual student. Whoever stamped them had a fuzzy ink pad.

A man of middle years who took himself rather seriously sauntered up to Lajos. "Where is she?" he asked.

"Coming," Lajos assured him, and glanced at me. I nodded. "Geel Yaytz, tis is Max Jungend. He is tah deprogrammer."

"Oh," I said, shaking his hand. "How nice—but I told you, the Techsci group took care of that themselves."

"Yes—but you cannot be too sure, can you, Max?"

"No, you certainly can't predict these things."

"So, I haf him jest in case."

"Well," I said, "I guess that makes good sense."

"Where is my girl?" he frowned at the door.

"Coming," I assured him. "Any minute."

"I am so happy, I am going to give you a check—"

He reached in his inside jacket breast pocket.

"Don't you want to wait until she comes?"

"No, no, you said she was coming. I belief

you—" he said, handing me the check—it was the full one-fifty, which I am embarrassed to say I kissed—right there in front of the studio publicist, the impressive press corps, the caterers, and Lajos' dearest and closest friends. I wasn't sure, but I thought I detected a girl-friend or two in the crowd.

His most impish oh-am-I-proud-of-myself smile crossed his liver spotted lips. "Just so you don't tink I am a complete fool—you see tose two musclemen at tah door?"

I looked, and I did. I nodded.

"Tey haf instructions not to let you out until I get my girl—and ten, I instruct tem not to let my baby out—"

"But then I can go?"

"Sure you can."

"With my check."

"Of course. You did tah job. You deserve tah payoff."

Too good to be true, I thought.

"Now, Yaytz, I want to haf some pictures with her when she comes—alone—I don't mean you hafn't earned tah right to be in tem."

I held up my hand. "Not to worry," I said. "I don't want publicity. I'm strictly low lock, stock and barrel."

"You mean low key, don't you?"

"Is that it?"

"In tis town, you know how important appear-ances are. And how do you make appearances? Wit peectures and copy."

I stood in awe of his inside knowledge.

266

Just then, Lajos' bosomy secretary with a stricken look of horror on her face announced, "The guest of honor," as she had been instructed to do.

Like a couple of amazon women from one of Lajos Bohem's world class flicks, Dawn and Sophie made their entrance. Dawn had cut her hair Mohawk and dyed it the most wonderful shade of orange. Her getup with chains and buckles, purple pants and chartreuse shirt would have been the envy of Michael Jackson, had Lajos thought to invite him. Her nose, eyebrows and ears looked pierced with rings and daggers, ball and chains.

Sophie had a see-through blouse showing rings piercing both breasts. Around her neck and arms were nail-studded black leather bands.

They were, as they say down at the optometrist's, a sight for sore eyeballs.

Flashbulbs were popping like there was no next week.

Dawn was taking it all in. She and Sophie were playing to the cameras shamelessly.

"Oh, Daddy," Dawn said, "it's so good to be back—this is my lover, Sophie—give her a big kiss, will you? She loves to be kissed by dirty old men, don't you Soph?"

Sophie nodded with enthusiasm, batting her eyelashes to beat the all girl orchestra. She presented her cheek to Lajos, but he recoiled in horror, though he couldn't keep from checking out her braless blouse.

She noticed him gawking and tore off her blouse. "Here, Lajos, want a better look?"

Straw wise, Lajos was at the end of his thread.

"Well, Daddy, I hope you kept my room just so for me and Sophie—we're back with bells on, and in spite of our past differences, it's forgive and forget time."

The press were furiously scribbling on their pads, the TV cameras glowing with red lights.

It was at this blessed juncture that I made my unnoticed exit, pretty much as we had planned it.

The taxi the girls had arranged was waiting for me just outside the gate. His meter was running and had racked up forty-five dollars so far—but I happily chalked it up to the cost of doing business.

First stop was the bank where I deposited the beautiful check and had one for twenty-five grand drawn in the name of Dawn Bohem, as promised, and left it in an envelope for her to pick up. She and Sophie were destined for a quiet spot in Hawaii, the precise locale undisclosed.

Then it was on home to face the music.

39

But there was no music at home. Tyranny was out as was her wont. I did the next best thing—went to the office.

"Will you look what the cat dragged in," was my greeting from my father-in-law. "Look at that hair, will you! Trying to ape a Latin lover are you, Malvin? So tell me, did it work? Attract any babes?"

"Carloads."

"Yeah, well I gotta tell you, I'm envious. I'd also like to tell you we missed you around here, but no such luck. Now why don't you see if you can produce something for a change?"

"Aye, aye, sir," I said, and saluted. In my mind, of course. Daddybucks was not long on a sense of humor.

I went home to water my palms and cycads. The triangle palms were showing some trunk and my *Encephalantos munchii* was starting a nice new set of leaves.

Inside, still no Tyranny—I called Doc D about my plants. When he came on the phone I commiserated, "a nasty business about your man, J. Kent Morgan," I said.

"Yeah—too bad—but I guess no one lives forever. Not even Morgan—"

"How will his passing affect the...group?"

"Oh, the ideas are strong. Stronger than any individual. It will carry on. Did your wife ever look into it?"

"I couldn't get her interested."

"Too bad. Done her a lot of good."

If it would have done her the same kind of good it did Lajos Bohem's wife, I figured we could count our blessings. After her recovery, Suzanne Bohem subsequently filed for divorce, got a nice settlement to minimize the adverse publicity, moved to Idaho and clerked in a ski/bike shop.

"Well, when can you bring the plants?" I asked the doc.

We set a time, but not before he sold me a couple more *chamael doreas*, a *Basselinia tomentosa*, and an excess of rather large and pricey cycads.

When I hung up, I thought about how whenever I'd finished one of my secret macho cases and returned to Tyranny Rex, I always feared I'd be in the Shitzu house. A guy who could stand up to the likes of Lajos Bohem and J. Kent Morgan could be afraid of his glass-blowing wife? I couldn't explain it. It was as though the fantasy world and the real world didn't connect. I was either one or the other.

I was relaxing on the living room lounge when Tyranny deigned to return to the homestead.

"Hi, Dorcas," I said.

"Oh," she was startled—"Malvin, is that you?"

Well, who else would it be? I wondered. She looked at me with a frown—I was waiting for her to comment on my dyed hair, but she didn't seem to notice.

"I'm sorry I was gone so long," I said—"took longer than I expected," I added vaguely.

"Oh," she said, her mind adrift, "were you gone?"

An Exerpt from

What Now, King Lear?

A Gil Yates Private Investigator Novel

by Alistair Boyle

She wanted to meet secretly—on neutral ground. Her husband had been murdered and there wasn't any reason to think she wouldn't be next. That was why I sat facing her on the sunny patio of a hotel restaurant in Bel Air—a locale not encumbered by the riffraff—a place whose door I had never, heretofore, darkened.

Pamela Sampson was she. The me is Gil Yates, private investigator. So private I am always astonished to get calls on my voice mail. I'm not listed. And that's not my real name. I had reason to hide my identity, and being named Malvin Stark was just one of them.

Orville Sampson had not been Pamela's first husband. She'd had two more of them—both recognizable names, which my canon of ethics prohibits me from mentioning.

One of Pamela's particular geniuses was to marry rich.

Another reason I hid my identity was my *modus operandi*—a nice, pretentious Latin phrase meaning mode of operation. It was taught to me by my boss and father-in-law, Elbert August Wempie, realtor, the gas bag's gas bag and the man who wrote the book on pretentiousness.

But at places like this Bel Air patio, some grounding in pretentiousness came in handy.

Pamela had deep dish dimples and wasn't lazy about cooking them up to sauce her wiles. She spoke not so much in sentences as in dimpled ideas.

"Stepchildren!" she said with a flourish of her napkin between her lap and lips. "The bane of my existence. *Especially* Orville's three daughters, *and* their husbands!" She made a face befitting an ill-fitting garment that threatened to cut off circulation to her vitals.

Pamela was eating some kind of lettuce concoction with a vinegary dressing on the side. I put her knocking at the door of fifty, so I was glad to see she was being kind to her vitals.

She wasn't about to sacrifice her svelte figure just because she was a widowed woman. *Especially* not because she was a widowed woman.

I was pleasantly chewing a pastrami on a fat French roll, the delectable juices coursing down my dewlaps.

"One of the kids did it," she said, dabbing a little vinegar from her mouth. "I'd bet my life on it."

"A girl would kill her father?" I asked, thinking of my own daughter, Felicity, and not wanting to believe.

"Well, not with her own hands. That was the thing about Sampson's daughters—they never had to get their hands dirty. Now their *husbands*—they've got hands just *made* for dirt."

"What attracted them?"

"Poor self-images—the poor girls were susceptible to anything in pants that came down the pike and looked at them cross-eyed. Mind you, I don't say their poor self-images were without foundation. To the person, they were losers, and popular cant to the contrary, likes do attract.

"It should be an easy job for you. You won't have to look further than the family," she said, as though a child could have divined that.

When I showed her by frown that I wasn't following her, she said, "Orville put oodles of money in trusts for his three daughters—let's not even *talk* about if they were worthy of it—now, he *controlled* those trusts during his lifetime. All they had to do was wait until he died and they'd have their grubby little hands on three hundred million or so, but no, they wanted more, sooner. He spent some of the income—peanuts, really, in the scheme of things. He bought me jewelry—he loved to do that." She flashed some diamond rings at me, but I didn't know much about the stuff. They say diamonds are forever, but if she isn't going to last forever, why give her a diamond?

"But what really frosted a couple of them was Orville's political donations to candidates they hated. Well, he *made* the money, after all, if he wanted to give the income to Attila the Hun, what business was it of theirs?

"Orville always said it was easy for his kids to hate his business-oriented candidates because the kids never earned a dollar on their own. Seemed to think the money was their birthright and the man who made it shouldn't be allowed to spend it."

"Any big gifts in the last year?"

"Not since they filed suit. It just killed him. They didn't need the gun and bullet, he was dying of a broken heart. He walked around like a zombie."

"I guess they were never close."

"Close? How close do you get to a man as dynamic as Orville? What attempts did they make?

Spoiled rotten," she did something with her nose and upper lip to indicate a bad smell.

"And, hey, Blue Eyes, I'm not trying to tell you he was a perfect father—how could he be when he was out making a billion bucks to put in their bank accounts? Well, I say it was the men put them up to it."

"Are the men the original husbands?"

"No. Second editions—each one. I can't say the firsts were any better. By the time the second courtships were beginning, they'd had their share of drug addictions, weight problems, mental disturbances, depression—the usual problems of the spoiled rich, and those, should I say inconveniences, took their toll."

Pamela looked me in the eye, giving me the feeling she was doing her own detective work on my trustworthiness. "There was this annoying clause in the will," she said, giving in to my purity of heart. "If Orville died in a crime, the criminal must be caught before anybody gets any money."

Clever, I thought. "But it didn't keep him from being murdered," I said. "Did he tell anyone?"

"Ah, there's the rub," she said. "He didn't tell me, and I'm sure he didn't tell the kids."

Not much of a deterrent, if he didn't tell anyone, I thought. "Didn't help," I said.

"Well, it puts pressure on us to find out. That's why I want to hire you—oh, don't get me wrong, I don't care about the money, I've got a nice allowance from the estate pending, blah, blah. I can stay in the house, travel, do anything I want. No, what I can't stand is loose ends, and this is the loosest. Besides, I can't stand those kids thinking I did it. Well, two of them, anyway; I assume the third knows who did it because *he* did it." She shook her head. "I still can't get used to it: Orville gone—once he was strong as an ox. Indestructible."

"What can you tell me about the kids' husbands?"

"Jason Q. Jackson is married to Francine, the oldest daughter. He was a plumber by trade, and I think they met when he was unplugging a toilet." She rolled her eyes. "Soooo romantic," she said, the sarcasm dripping from her dimples. "He's built like a moose. Of course, now he's an entrepreneur."

"Doing what?"

"God knows. Anything he can get his hands on that has as close to a zero chance for success as you can come.

"Then there's lovely Kurt B. Roberts. You wouldn't think he was a pathological liar to look at him. Quite presentable, really. Short, even in his elevator shoes. He was a chiropractor—he has the annoying habit of putting one hand under his chin, the other on the back of his head and jerking his head to one side in polite society—snapping his backbone with a great cracking sound."

"Does he still practice?"

"Heavens no, why should he? I think they met when he manipulated Lolly's back. It was a tiny step to manipulating her psyche. He's a real estate mogul now—the riskier the venture, the more he salivates. Kurt didn't join the lawsuit—just instigated it, then backed off to ingratiate himself with Orville. Too clever by half. If they win, he benefits. It's a no-risk deal."

"How did the other two meet?"

"Rolf was an auto mechanic. Fixed Brenda's car and her in the backseat—right in the shop." She shook her head. "No accounting for taste," she said wistfully.

"Whose? His or hers?"

"Both," she said. "But that was the thing about the marriages—the men saw the obvious dollar signs. God knows what the girls saw."

"What's the mechanic's last name?"

"Gorberg. Rolf Gorberg."

"What about your husband? What kind of guy was he?"

Her eyes misted over—I thought it was an expression of genuine sentiment.

"I loved him, Mr. Yates. With all I had. He could be an S.O.B., but I saw through the bluster. He came from nothing. I wasn't rich in my youth, but I was royalty compared to him. I mean, my father was a postman and my mother took in washing."

"Well," I said, surprised at the admission, "you've done well—"

"Darn right, I've done well, but I earned everything I got by the sweat of my brow. You know how many women in my circumstances marry wealthy men?"

"No, I..."

"And I've had *three*."

"What's the secret?" I asked.

"There is no secret," she said, "only enthusiasm.

I'm sorry...You asked what kind of guy Orville was. Let me tell you a story by way of explanation: We had a serious drought in Bel Air some years ago and the city put in a water moratorium and a fine for anyone who used water in excess of their stringent allotment. Mr. Sampson's fine was thirty-five thousand dollars for the two hottest months. He paid it. 'I like grass,' he said. Grass wasn't the only thing that man liked. He liked wealth, power, women—the order depending on his mood.

"He'd had two prior marriages—both very successful for a couple of years. As he got older, his wives got younger. His employees (there were just shy of eighteen thousand of them) used to joke behind his back that if this behavior kept up, the old man would exit this life in the arms of his twelve-year-old bride.

"He was in the papers all the time. He was a maverick, a buccaneer. Very colorful. He settled three hundred and fifty million bucks on each of his three daughters. Of course, there was a catch. The money was put in trust for the girls to get it out of Sampson's already overburdened larder. It was a tax dodge. Let's say the bulk of the corpus, as the lawyers say, was in tax free bonds. That luscious income would be tax free. And Sampson could have it for his own while he was alive. When he croaked, the girls would get a considerable slice of the pie.

"But now two of the girls, or perhaps, their husbands got a little antsy, as they say, for verily it is said, what good is three hundred and fifty million if you can't touch it, feel it, smell it, or spend it? Besides, what if the old man outlived them? Confucius say more fun to spend money while alive.

"Sampson thought so, too. And he was, if he did say so himself, a world class spender. He was one of those rare birds who not only knew how to make money, but also how to spend it. 'Stimulates the economy,' he used to say—'and also stimulates the hell out of me.'"

Pamela's eyes were awash with tears.

"The unspoken fear here," she said, "is...am I going to be next? I've already caught the vibes that the kids aren't happy with the provisions in the will that include me."

My eyebrows went flying. "Three hundred and fifty million each isn't enough?"

"When it comes to Orville's kids," she said. "Human greed knows no bounds."